MAD
PRAIRIE

FLANNERY
O'CONNOR
AWARD
FOR
SHORT
FICTION

MAD PRAIRIE

STORIES AND
A NOVELLA
BY

Kate McIntyre

THE UNIVERSITY OF
GEORGIA PRESS
ATHENS

Published by the University of Georgia Press
Athens, Georgia 30602
www.ugapress.org
© 2021 by Kate McIntyre
All rights reserved
Designed by Kaelin Chappell Broaddus
Set in 9.5/13.5 Dolly Pro Regular by Kaelin Chappell Broaddus

Printed and bound by Sheridan Books, Inc.
The paper in this book meets the guidelines for permanence
and durability of the Committee on Production Guidelines for
Book Longevity of the Council on Library Resources.

Most University of Georgia Press titles are
available from popular e-book vendors.

Printed in the United States of America
21 22 23 24 25 P 5 4 3 2 1

Library of Congress Cataloging-in-Publication Data
Names: McIntyre, Kate, 1982– author.
Title: Mad prairie : stories and a novella / by Kate McIntyre.
Description: Athens : The University of Georgia Press, [2021] |
Series: Flannery O'Connor award for short fiction
Identifiers: LCCN 2021018805 | ISBN 9780820360744 (paperback) |
ISBN 9780820360751 (ebook)
Subjects: LCGFT: Short stories.
Classification: LCC PS3613.C54256 M33 2021 | DDC 813/.6—dc23
LC record available at https://lccn.loc.gov/2021018805

To Pam McIntyre
and John McIntyre

CONTENTS

MAD
PRAIRIE

Prairie Vision

WE'LL HERD THE LOVED ONES from the tents to a low fence to present a live feed of the mine courtesy of Prairie Vision, the TV station I own, or rather, used to own. I had to step aside due to a perceived conflict of interest when I was elected governor. My advisor Eddie held that some suspicious SOBs might say a state politician shouldn't also run the only regional news outlet. Nuts to Eddie. Luckily, the good folks at Prairie Vision (our tagline: "Prairie Vision: See Further") still do what I like.

Eddie's always trying to smooth my edges. He doesn't understand that people want a hard-liner. My appeal lies in my sure-footed climb from nothing to a pile of money. That's what put me in the governor's mansion, despite my Latino last name. The mighty dollar matters more than anything, and that's the bottom line. It's fair, somehow. Pure. My little brother, Manny, never understood, and I wish he would have. Things could have turned out differently for him.

As my wife, Jennie, and I and Eddie and a few other staffers pull up in our bulletproof SUV, I see the rescuers have slapped up the state flag on a bluff behind us. I'm in navy because it tones down the red in my cheeks. Eddie said to wear black for gravitas but on my big day I don't figure to look like a goddamned undertaker, like I should be passing out mints to mourners blubbering into each other's coat sleeves. I'll grasp this tragedy by the short hairs. I'm wearing cowboy boots to show I'm like everybody. Not my ostrich or lizard boots, but plain cow leather, the pair I had Eddie wear until the toes turned up. You can't fake that sort of authenticity.

Jennie's in something boring, a shell-pink suit cut high so it de-emphasizes her tits, plus flats as a nod to the rocky terrain. She looks womanly, maternal even. You'd never guess she used to be a ring girl for a semi-pro-wrestling league down in Wichita.

I'm delighted at how sexy everything is. The rescuers hustle about in hard hats like little penis caps. The dirt around the hole flushes shades of flesh: red, beige, and tan. The hole itself gapes wide for the rescue capsule. Even folks who don't care for human drama and the possibility of live televised death enjoy pornography.

I take my place for the photo op in front of the state flag, which features a field being plowed by a team of oxen. Our state motto flaps above it: *Ad astra per aspera* (To the Stars through Difficulties), which I wanted to amend to *Ad terra per aspera* (To the Earth through Difficulties), but Eddie said no one would get it. I said, hell yes, they would. They could Google it like I did.

I don a gold hard hat. Everyone else's is yellow. Strapped at my side is my pistol, a Desert Eagle with a special pavé inlay across the barrel that reads, "The Guv." It was gifted to me by some fellows in a citizens' rights organization, in appreciation of the recent loosening of open-carry restrictions I'd shepherded through the state senate. Sweat pours down my calves into my cowboy boots. It won't show. My face is hot in the sun. I don't squint.

I stop by the loved ones' tents. There was a memo about grooming, and I'm glad to see the salon staff has buffed and polished and hosed down and trimmed the loved ones. The plan is to invite the most photogenic folks past the barricades, right up to the mouth, where the joyous reunion will be documented by Prairie Vision. Why this insistence on excellent personal appearance? Pride. If the citizenry looks great, that can only help me. I want the broadcast to set coastal elites back on their heels, show that we midwesterners are just like them, albeit slightly more slow-tongued and doughy.

My state has gotten some bad press lately, what with the school shooting and then the revelation of the diary of the young killer with his piss-poor grammar and punctuation. Some see it as an indictment of my tiny little cuts to K–12, but that savings allowed us to repave I-70 from Topeka to KC. A smoother ride you'll never find, even if you aren't cruising in a big SUV like mine. That brought out the grumps, too. Why, they moaned, does the governor have a whole fleet of SUVs? Shouldn't he pick something more environmentally friendly? I added to the stable a truly massive pickup fueled by biodiesel, which gets forty-two miles per gallon.

Now I pose with my foot on the lip of the hole. I tell myself, "Hope, seriousness, dignity." The mine smell drifts up—wet limestone and dirt. It rocks me forward on my toes. Good vibes from that pit, like I'll find what I want.

I always reckoned those trapped miners were alive. Call it a sixth sense for the soil. After my many years underground, I've got a direct line through the roots of the tallgrass and sunflowers that dot the prairie, through the rich glacial soil deposits that make us such an ag power-house, down into the bedrock.

I figured that folks would tune in. Though I look like a young man, I was already in my teens when Baby Jessica tumbled down that old well in Texas. The flashing ambulance lights and strained voices of the news crews wondering if the little darling would live through her ordeal: that slow pageantry left its mark. Never did I think I'd have the opportunity to administer my own tragedy. Administer in the sense of supervise. I had nothing to do with getting those boys stuck down there, but damn if I won't yank them back out.

The mine is mine, too. Did I mention that? I invested in top-of-the-line safety and security. Don't know what happened. It's enough to make a lesser man cry sabotage, start wondering about recent gang activity in the area. La Cuchilla out of Wichita, specifically.

That mine makes up a not insubstantial part of my fortune. After I bought it, I set to work looking for a use for its halite. Salt is cheap. But then I considered how this was the only mine of its kind in the whole country, and how the salt was a beautiful mint green due to chromium impurities, very distinctive, and thus, Flint Hills Artisanal Salt was born. Chefs love fancy shit, so I sell it to them for twenty times the price of your standard table salt. The previous owners were Hollywood dudes who used the mine for storage of classic film reels, renting it out to studios at a very tidy price per square foot. I kept that up when I bought them out. Apparently, while salt eats away the miners' throats, it has the opposite effect on film, preserving it forever. My trapped men had been digging out farther passages because the current ones were full of Shirley Temple and Rin Tin Tin, Myrna Loy and William Powell. Funny to think of all those stars under a wheat field.

<center>~~~~~</center>

The Prairie Vision cameras zoom in on the spot where miners' faces will emerge. Guess how many pairs of eyeballs will view the broadcast of the poor miners' stumble toward the light? About five billion worldwide. Five oh-oh-oh-oh-oh-oh-oh-oh. Take off just one of those zeros, and that's how many dollars I've got. But I digress. I would gladly give each viewer a shiny quarter to say thank you for his support. Two quarters, even: one per eyeball. A bad deal for pirates!

Of course, I couldn't put my hands on so many quarters at the moment because, just between you and me, I've got this funny feeling the economy is just about fucked, if the state budget is any sign. That's why I've been hiding heavy gold bars all around the governor's mansion, just in case Jennie and I and the kids need to amscray pronto some night. I made a treasure map of what's kept where, and the great side benefit of having the gold on site is that I can test the honesty of my staff. They know I watch them.

"Eddie!" I say, jerking my foot back from the edge of the shaft, triggering a small cave-in. He scrabbles to my side, temples sweating. "Eddie," I say, "I want to pull the miners the last few feet myself, so that they land in my arms."

"The issue with that, Governor," Eddie says, "is the rescue pod weighs two tons." He raises his Muppet-like hands helplessly.

"Perhaps if Jennie helped, if we enlisted Bryce and Terry," I say, flexing so the suit sleeves pull taut. Bryce and Terry are my two strong children, just a phone call away at peewee football scrimmage.

"The engineers say we have to use the winch," Eddie says. "We don't want to drop the miners back down the shaft."

I accept this with good grace. I'll be right on the scene, the second person each miner will embrace after their most attractive loved one. First would be better, but I'm reasonable. Maybe one miner will choose to fall into my arms instead of his mother's or girlfriend's. I suggest to Eddie that some stage directions could be whispered through the underground cable, into the miners' ears. He winks.

wMMm

The story of the miners is my story, really. Let me take you back to a deprived childhood, for we were poor as shit. I never knew my father, the rat, whose only contribution to my and Manny's life besides some chromosomes and melanin was our last name, which has come in handy only twice: one time as a teen, and then in election season, when the name attracted Latino votes despite my policies. It cut both ways, of course, losing me ground with the white racists, but then my good looks and lack of mastery of the Spanish language factored in, too, so it turned into a wash or maybe a slight net positive. I was not unpalatable to many voters. Not quite a majority, but many. "They love you," my mother roared into my chest the night I won.

My mother, bless her, did her best with me and Manny. She had me when she was just fifteen. It was inevitable that we'd slide into the Airliner Motel on Pacific Avenue, for twenty bucks a week in advance, settling onto yellow mattresses beside a yowling air conditioner that leaked gray water on the brown carpet. The walls were nicotine brown from generations of cigarette smokers, and Ma did her part to help darken them, as did I, once I turned twelve. Manny was eight years younger than me. Ma claimed we shared a father, though I don't know if that's true. She never brought a father type around the motel, which was smart of her. I would have kicked his ass.

Ma worked every night at an establishment next door called Pirate Booty, a buccaneer-themed titty bar. It had a neon sign with a parrot who nudged open a treasure chest with his beak. Inside the chest were long ladies' legs that kicked up piles of gold coins. Manny and I would sit on the curb by a dumpster and watch the sign for hours. Money and women, and women and money. Ma claimed she was just a waitress, but she came home with crumpled wads of ones. One night she was crying, a bruise ringing her left eye. When she saw me, she brought her hand to my face and told me the world was better elsewhere, that I should always remember I had every right to the best things in life, and there was no shame in going after them.

Manny never made it out of the underclass like I did. He was too thoughtful, too stubborn. I tried to tempt him away from his low-paying job, but he never answered my calls or voicemails. A proud fellow. You think looks don't matter? See this photo of me and Manny at nineteen and eleven. Me with my strong nose, jutting cheekbones, stature, and Manny with his soft chin, round cheeks, petulant lips. The lips of a spoiled boy who was unwilling to compromise with an unjust system to get ahead. And my lips: thin, sure, manly. Our destinies etched on our faces.

wwww

Everyone waits so eagerly for the mine capsule to ascend. The rescuers pace with tools in their fists, looking for something to fix. My fear is that in their zeal they'll adjust something they shouldn't, and the capsule will careen down the shaft. Jennie sighs and shifts, and Eddie rushes to bring her a chair. He holds her hand a moment longer than he needs to. She pats his thigh.

Now the first miner rises up in the pod. There's a long moment when the men with tools wrangle the shining tube. The door swings open, achingly slow. The miner's child weeps. And there he is, curled in the arms of paramedics. Eddie, Jennie, and I spent last night poring over pictures of the miners, picking who'd ascend first. We settled on the handsomest, and the crying kid is gravy. His wife removes his hard hat so that the cameras can more easily capture the charming features. His hair is limp, but his jaw is powerful. The reporters explain that his name is Raúl López and he misses his mother's chorizo empanadas. I grasp his hand and whisper, "Write a book fast, if you want my advice."

He stares past me. He wilts back onto the stretcher. I grab his limp arm and wave his hand at the crowd. They cheer. I don't want to let go but the paramedics make me.

wwww

The other time my last name helped: One morning when I was fifteen, while Manny and I were taking turns exploding out of the dumpster at the Airliner, trying to scare each other, a pickup truck with a bunch of young men in the back pulled up. They looked like us. The driver asked my name and if I wanted to work, and I said yes and gave him my name, first and last, and a good thing, too, because that last name got me on the truck. Manny tried to join me, but the driver told him no; he was too small. Manny's top lip rose to his nose, a prelude to tears. "Don't you cry, Manny," I shouted. I settled into the bed, refused to look back as the truck pulled away. The guys all were talking Spanish. I just smiled and nodded.

We headed south on back roads for twenty minutes or so, through fields of milo and wheat and bare prairie, until we arrived at the salt mine. I got loaded up: a hard hat with a light and battery pack, a self-rescuer. The conditions were tough. You'd expect it to be cool inside, but no. The air was hot, and so dry and salty that it took only a week before I was coughing up blood. Some of the miners who had been at it longer had pink teeth from the blood in their throats. I got paid forty dollars weekly, tax-free, but five dollars went straight to La

Cuchilla for protection. The men in the gang impressed me greatly, even as I hated them. They wore alligator boots with the snouts still on, leather pants, and shiny shirts richly patterned with designs of gold nuggets, chains, and jasmine flowers. They had extravagant tattoos—crowns, crossed spears, names in Gothic script, and eagles with snakes in their beaks.

One of the miners taught me a song about them, and we'd sing it to each other. I got him to do a rough translation:

> Beware La Cuchilla,
> They'll come for you!
> Beware La Cuchilla,
> They're after you!
>
> They come with their guns,
> They cut with their knives,
> They slash with their machetes,
> And they want to start a fight.
>
> Beware La Cuchilla,
> They like to watch you sleep.
> Don't go out at night,
> Lest La Cuchilla string you up!

Manny got older. He started at the mine, too. On our days off, we'd loll in puddles in the motel parking lot. When we saw clouds forming, we laid ourselves in dips in the pavement, telling stories about our future while the rain beat our faces. We knew so little of the world. Manny said he'd leave Kansas and never return. He wanted to run his hands over the mosaics at Pompeii, dance on a floor that lit up, eat a coconut fresh from a palm tree, and shake hands with a monkey. He wanted to be very tall and not to have to do any more bending or digging. He had knobby knees that popped out of joint if he wasn't careful and warts on his hands that the doctor said came from gnawing at his fingernails like a nervous rabbit. That's how infection gets in. My fingernails, it should not need to be said, are immaculate.

I didn't mind bending or digging in the mine the way Manny did, so long as I could have a fine pair of alligator boots. Now I own a closet full, with snouts of all sizes and peering glass eyes. I can't wear them in public, more's the pity, because the animal-rights fuckers would give me hell. Manny got his wish, too. The part about no more digging, anyway.

The family of the second miner, Billy Bartow, describes him as "a person who loves parties." Jubilant, he raises a cheer from deep in the hole. He has brought us presents. Can you guess what? A bucket of salt from the mine. These chunks are treated with great reverence for the cameras. The rescuers hold them in eager fingers, hopeful that the cameras might pan up to their looks of awe, such handsome faces behind the anonymity of the jumpsuits. Billy hands me a rock, and I kiss it and hoist it above my head to applause.

My mother didn't like her boys working at the mine, but we didn't like her working at Pirate Booty, either, so we were square. I kept in mind her words of advice about how I didn't deserve any less than anyone else, and it wasn't long before I confronted my mine bosses with evidence of their labor violations—safety procedures and hiring practices, tax stuff. I stuck it to them, with Manny to back me up, though neither of us cut a very imposing figure, at twenty-three and fifteen. Manny had dropped out of school by then. I'd explained to the bosses I'd only feel content if they gave me a portion of their own wages each week. I enjoyed the hundredfold salary increase for several months before I sensed that their patience had stretched so thin they might kill me. Then, I turned them in, and the grateful mine owners, whose hands had never touched raw halite, who never felt the burn of mineral salt in their nostrils, whose blood was not in the mine, as mine was, gave me even more money.

The third miner, Juan Torres, falls as the pod door swings wide. His face, which Prairie Vision's high-definition cameras swivel toward, is pale as a lizard's belly. Two strong men in their jumpsuits hoist him up and bundle him into the ambulance. There is a red smear on one man's shoulder where Juan's mouth was. I stab at my own shoulder to show him the imperfection, but Eddie is confused and goes after me with a handkerchief, intent to rub away the phantom stain.

All these Latino names might get you wondering about labor practices. I know that game. The papers are all in order, impeccable. Tattling on the mine bosses got my friends deported, which I felt awful about, so hiring migrants now is a little way to even the score.

God help me. There's a lot of atoning to do.

wwww

The miners' crisis, I must admit, arrived at just the right time. Despite all the stuff I've got going for me—my wealth, my kindness, my success in the recent election (in which I received 48.6 percent of the vote)—no one likes me. My economic policies (big old tax cuts, aggressive privatization so the free market can do its good work) have been described as "bizarrely inhumane" and "downright wrongheaded." I got booed at a college basketball game. My popularity rating was in the crapper, and suddenly the miners were buried, so my thought was, why not bring both up at once? The initial reports gave the miners a slim chance to live. There were twenty-two of them stuck down there, and if they had made it to the safety room, a big if, they would have six square feet of living space per person. Which is not enough. I measured it out in my office. Did you know that's only 2.4 feet each way?

I gave rousing speeches about the miners' inevitable survival, about our duty to these poor trapped men. And never once did I doubt. True leadership, I'll say in the book about myself that I'm itching to start writing, is this: surety in one's rightness, even in the face of all evidence to the contrary. My approval rating is at 54 percent now, up twenty points from just a month ago. Already I've got my fingers crossed for another disaster. Not another mining one. A minor one.

шшш

But wait, I still haven't told you the whole truth and nothing but. It's important to get this recorded accurately, because someday my term will end and my second autobiography must be written. I have jotted several titles already in a calfskin notepad I keep close to my heart: *Up from the Underground: The Adventure of an Uncommon Common Man; This Land Is Your Land, This Land Is Mine Land: A Poor Lad's Improbable Journey to Places of Power and Privilege; Salt of the Earth, Salt from the Earth; From the Mines to the Stars, through Difficulties.*

The whole truth is that I keep a small box of Flint Hills Artisanal Salt in the drawer of my nightstand, and sometimes when my wife is asleep I flick my tongue through it and swallow the crystals down with scotch. I remember my brother. And, yes, I cry. Manny isn't with us now. Though I wonder. In fact, I swear, once late at night, my tongue burning, my eyes burning too, Manny came to me. From the shadows under the bed, he uncoiled like a cobra. That soft boy now a tall, well-muscled man. I knew my brother. He knew me. He grinned. His hair fell back to show the gore. The AC shuddered on and he left with the cool dry wind. It pains me to say more.

шшш

Another thing I should probably mention, just to be thorough: the first thing I did after my election was deputize some old pals, call them "volunteer lawmen," give them shiny gold badges (they already had guns), and set them on the track of La Cuchilla. Preying on such weak people, miners and the like, made the gang, in turn, vulnerable, without resources. Middle-aged, slow, and alone, without anyone to miss them. The noses of their alligator boots were so worn the stuffing showed. Today they are still housed in a prison in a secret location. They are treated well.

After the inauguration, I moved my mother to a big new house in a neighborhood called Mariposa Heights. She's having the time of her life gardening in minishorts, hosting loud daiquiri parties on the patio. The neighbors, doctors and lawyers, know not to complain if they want internships for their sons and daughters.

wmm

Now the miners emerge in a regular rhythm, like goods on an assembly line. Every time the pod door opens, the crowd oohs and aahs. My back, touchy from so much pickaxing in my youth, seizes as I stoop over the stretchers. I no longer want to scoop up each man and carry him to the ambulance, like a groom sweeping his bride across a threshold. I settle for some hearty shoulder pats.

Bent over the man the earth has coughed up most recently, I stiffen. He's got Manny's face. Those eyebrows that nearly meet above his nose, his big dark eyes, his full lips—all there before me. A weird strangled gasp catches in my throat. The body was never found. I had hoped always Manny might be alive, but never did I suspect that I'd uncover my brother just where I'd lost him, all those years ago.

I grasp the man's shoulders. The man turns his head and the illusion—a trick of the fading light—is dispelled. A birthmark the shape and hairiness of a tarantula disfigures the miner's cheek. This man is no Manny. I want to kick him, but that wouldn't be proper, so instead I bite my cheek until my teeth meet. I swallow before baring my teeth for the cameras.

wmm

I lied about La Cuchilla being treated well. After they were captured, some alive, some dead, some somewhat alive, I planned to hold a press conference about what I did to them, to release pictures of the disgraced gang members, their faces spat on, their heads stomped by volunteer deputies' boots. But those are not the images that should be shown, Eddie reminded me. And he's right, of course. More photos of children with robots they made despite cuts to education, more farmers looking pleased with themselves, riding high on tractors in fields of waving golden wheat. Fewer mangled noses, mouths blubbering for mercy, though Kansas citizens are tough on crime, and most, I feel sure, would want to see the gang members' skulls cracked, the silk shirts stained beyond the skills of even the most adept dry cleaner. Nearly all of us are doomed to lives that are foregone conclusions because of the circumstances of our births. That's why I'm a fan of small government.

~~~

Even today, down in the holding area where we keep La Cuchilla, a volunteer deputy with a brass badge flays the skin from the forearms of several gang members, telling them the pain will stop when they reveal what became of Manny. He wasn't found in the mine; he never emerged. He must be somewhere, and La Cuchilla must tell me. If not, the skin will be allowed to heal and then stripped again. I think he's still in the mine.

~~~

The miner Bernardo Guerrero is up next, a bald sixty-two-year-old with hungry eyes. His body is vole-like. I don't like his look. There is a nice moment when he meets a daughter—illegitimate—for the first time. His wife stands to one side scowling at his toddler. Jennie goes and has a word with the wife, who puts on a smile even scarier than her grimace. The sweet scene makes me eager to see Manny again. How will he have changed? What stories will he have to share?

~~~

I should explain about my last night in the mines. You'll probably ask yourself, because of course you've read my first autobiography, *A Good Man for the Job*, "Why hasn't he told us what it was like down in the mines? He knows better than anybody what the trapped miners are thinking!" It hurts me to discuss it, because I lost my brother in the mine.

One night after Manny and I had quit our jobs, he and I returned to meet with the owners, in from California. A large payment was due, and I was eager to see whether the mine had kept up safety standards. Manny had been shaking before the meeting, and already I regretted asking him to join me. We'd both been drinking. The mine owners grumbled loudly about the price of my silence, which, I will admit, was steep, but them's the breaks. It was what I believed the market could bear. They seemed nervous, scuffing their feet and dimming and brightening their headlamps. Soon we found out why: a La Cuchilla assassin lurked in a side tunnel. He sneaked up behind us while the fat owner told a story about a goat who wouldn't stop eating until his stomach exploded. I was so busy figuring out the hidden message (I believe it had to do with greed) that I didn't hear the goon. He clouted Manny on the head and would have done the same to me had I not fled. A purely logical interpretation is that Manny was killed in the mine. I don't believe that.

The world was too bad for Manny, too loud and venal and difficult. This is my world, not his. One time when he was in junior high, he ended up with a concussion after a fight in the hallway. I asked him what happened, and he said he was trying to stand up for some white girl. "Fight for yourself first and only!" I urged him, but he just shook his head, his purple-rimmed eyes those of a much older man. At the Airliner, he'd crawl into a corner far from the TV, pull a bedspread over his head, clap his wart-covered hands over his ears, and rock. I think he's found an even quieter hiding spot.

wmm

Hours pass, and just as the sun dips toward the flat horizon, shading the whole sky orange, the last miner ascends. My entire staff and most of the reporters have sunken into chairs, though I still pace and rally the crowd that, too, has diminished, as loved ones follow their miners to medical facilities. Now the scene is mine. It's as if I am giving birth, as if I myself am the mine, and the miners are emerging in that penis-shaped pod from my womb. A confusing image, but powerful.

Poor Domingo Rojas. All the reporters know of him is that he takes medicine for hypertension, "according to his ex-wife." He arrives vomiting, his face bulging, eyes screwed shut. Watery gray bile has sprayed his shirt, and everyone backs up, except for me.

I kiss him on both cheeks, my own sore from smiles. I whisper in his ear: "Where is Manny? He's still down there, yes? The tunnel system of La Cuchilla is even more complicated than I thought, right?" His head shakes—maybe a nod. The ambulance drivers wheel him away. I can't object too strenuously because the cameras are on me, and Eddie watches from a lawn chair. Bear in mind your gravitas, his expression indicates. His attitude strikes me as a bit too free.

Just as the ambulance door is about to close, I hear a weak cry from the miner, and I rush toward him. "Uno más!" he says. "Hay otro, hay otro." His eyes roll sideways; his body heaves and stills.

Of course there's another. All this time I've known it.

Eddie tugs my coat, but I bat him away. Jennie observes with grim reserve, as if at last I'm justifying her concerns. They sit together, Jennie's hand in Eddie's blazer pocket. Eddie smiles strangely. The last few loved ones board the shuttle buses, mouths agape, teeth agleam. As I reach the hole, the rescuers stumble over each other, no longer sure of the script. The cameras roll on. I hop in the capsule and command the men to send me down. I'll grab my brother by the scruff of his neck to haul him up to the light. Everyone will see what I've done for him. What great TV we'll make. The shaft is too dark. I'm not afraid. A gust from below fills my pants. I touch the grip of my pistol. I raise my hand to wave, but nobody's watching.

The Moat

IN EARLY MARCH OF Vern and Della's eighth year of marriage, Vern lost his job as demolition technician at the limestone quarry. After the supervisor told him the news, he scooped up his hard hat, thermos, lunch pail, and harness, cussing and kicking his way out to his truck. He found Della at home in the kitchen cooking a batch of jam. Della took one look at him, dusty and hangdog, stubbly and limp-armed, and knew the other shoe had dropped.

"Those idiots at A&B finally let me go," he told her. She supposed she should let him lay his head on her breasts while she ran her fingers through his wispy blond hair, but she'd just added the pectin. The jam required constant stirring at this delicate stage. Also, Vern deserved to get canned. He'd bragged about how he'd kicked the supervisor's shed each time he walked past and dropped pinches of quarry grit into the other workers' lunch pails. When he told her these things, she'd nodded in sympathy. Vern wasn't a man you questioned.

"What am I going to do now?" Vern asked. He stood with his hands on his hips, his lower lip puffed out the way their son Harland did his when he was frustrated. Della shook her head and eyed the bubbling jam. The quarry was all Vern knew.

Vern and Della had met at the quarry. She had done payroll in the shed and watched the men break rock. The supervisor said that the men who did Vern's job were either the dumbest or the bravest. Della used to think Vern was the bravest.

When Della got pregnant, Vern made her quit her job. She didn't want to, but he said he'd take care of her, and at nineteen, she found that beautiful. Maybe if she'd still been at the quarry she could have kept an eye on him, tamped down his rough moods, and they'd have two paychecks rather than zero.

The jam was ready to pour, but Della kept stirring. Vern's eyes followed her, daring her to say something. Silently, Della stirred. She'd had this same feeling on her wedding day—another situation Vern had sullied. It was a fury too big to be contained in her body. If she spoke now, she'd never stop. Her words would blow Vern's hair back and send him sprawling out of her kitchen so she could pour her damn jam before it spoiled. She didn't speak. Vern wandered out.

She made a mental list of all of the good things about Vern: he didn't have problems with alcohol, he never beat the children, he didn't waste money at the dog track or speedway, he used to be very attractive, he was the only family she had left besides the boys now that her dad was gone. Della's father hadn't liked Vern. He said that once you stripped away the fine blond hair, flayed the sunburned skin, and teased off the stringy muscle, all that remained was fear. That was true of everyone she knew.

wWMm

Della and Vern and their boys, Harland and Mylan, lived on Old Highway 40, after the town petered out to squat, rambling country houses and after the country houses themselves thinned. The nearest house was a couple miles away, not even in shouting distance. They had a seven-room ranch house and detached garage on five acres. Heart cutouts on the shutters. New vinyl siding. The yard dotted with Harland and Mylan's Tonka trucks and Big Wheels and squirt guns. Vern's half-ton Chevy in the gravel drive. Vern built the garage. His tools gleamed on the walls. The garage leaned.

Vern spent hours outside now that he was laid off, digging weeds from the deep-green, close-cropped lawn using an icepick in their wedding pattern. Their bank balance sloughed away, but he refused to look for another job. Della tried to make suggestions, but nothing suited Vern. He'd shake his head as Della read ads from the employment section of the *Salina Journal*: carpet shampooer, light duty lube technician, over-the-road flatbed driver. Vern read the paper, too, though he was more interested in the crime blotter.

Finally, he applied for seasonal work as a silo washer (dangling three stories, volatile wheat particles blowing up his nose, the power sprayer vibrating away thoughts—just up Vern's alley, Della reckoned), but they said he was too old.

Della was returning from a jam delivery in town one day when Vern waved her over to the lawn where he knelt. Limp weeds and sheets of newspaper ringed him, sending up a sharp green odor and the old-tire smell of ink. "A woman was raped in town this week. Also, somebody broke into a truck and stole the stereo. I sure would miss my stereo," he said, pointing the icepick right at her. He picked dirt off the grape design in the handle.

"That poor woman," Della said. "Have they found the man who did it?"

"Nope, they haven't. Yet another reason you shouldn't be getting over to Salina alone. You're too cute," he told her. "And not very strong."

Della objected to that last bit. She'd been hoisting jam pots long enough now that her arm muscles were hard. But Vern was underfoot so much, and there was so very much jam to make and only so much time in the day, so she said, "Maybe you could do a few deliveries. Get some air, see some folks. Someone might even have a lead on a job."

Vern grunted.

Della quickly told him, "Well, you don't have to look for work right now. I'll be your sugar mama." She could up her production to three, four hundred jars a week. Maybe put it in smaller jars. The folks who bought her jam at her friend Crystal's store, Homespun Happiness, were passing the jam on—gifts for neighbors, pastors, mailmen. Crystal said people weren't looking for a good price per ounce but a nice presentation. Maybe she was right.

"How are you going to take care of the kids when you're swanning off to town every other minute?" Vern said.

Lately Della felt like she wasn't dealing with a man but with a sick animal. Better just to let it crawl in a corner and lick its wounds. No need to make it do something against its instinct. The boys were fine.

But Della couldn't help herself. "What's the problem now?" she said.

"I'm sad, Della. I ain't got a purpose anymore," Vern said. "The supervisor said I was good for nothing and he knew I had been since the day he hired me. Twelve years and he says that."

"Oh, Vern," Della said. She touched his shoulder. He shrugged her off.

"I don't need sympathy. I just thought that was real crappy."

He did this often, pissed her off then made her feel sorry for him. It worked, even though she could see it coming from a mile off.

Della said, "You've taken care of us for such a long time, is all I'm saying. Everyone deserves a break."

wwww

In May, two months after Vern lost his job, Della ladled sour cherry preserves into sterilized jars. Vern stood over her asking if she hadn't perhaps overcooked this batch. The boys arrived home from school and peered in the kitchen warily. Lately Vern had turned affectionate, scooping them up and hugging too hard. If they saw him, they bolted. She wished she were as agile as her sons. Today she told the boys to come in. They were a couple of round, solid children, towheaded like their daddy. In the winter, they bundled into puffy coats, Kansas City Chiefs for Harland, and camouflage print for Mylan. In the summer, they wore T-shirts printed with robots or eagles and American flags and shorts with elasticized waists. Their eyelids didn't even have creases yet. Now she squatted to hug them, burrowing her nose deep in Mylan's hair, which smelled of sweetgrass and baby shampoo. She asked how their day had gone, and Harland told her, "I've got to build a diorama. A castle."

"Well," Della said, "that sounds like something your father could help with. He's so handy. What do you say, Vern?"

Vern was always awkward with compliments. He stood a few feet away. "Yep, son. I reckon I could help you out." Della's shoulders relaxed. "Let's go take a browse in those encyclopedias while your mother gets dinner on the table." The boys and their father trooped down to the basement to dig out the C volume from a 1981 *World Book Encyclopedia*, inherited from Vern's uncle. His cousins hadn't wanted the set when Vern's uncle had passed. Illiterate, Della suspected.

Vern and the boys stormed the stairs when Della called them to dinner, abuzz with talk of turrets and battlements and lances and trebuchets (also known as catapults, they told her) and bows and arrows and chain mail and towers. And moats.

Vern, breathing hard from the climb, pointed at Della. "She's our queen," he announced to the boys. "I'm the king and you two are knights gallant."

Harland pointed at Mylan and said, "I think he should be the squire." Their father laughed and punched Harland on the shoulder. Harland jumped, his eyes welling.

"Right, and our house is our castle," Della said quickly, rolling her eyes but smiling to make sure Vern knew she was just kidding.

"Yep," Vern said, "our house is my castle."

"I'm glad to see you all are making progress," Della told the boys. "I think I'll cook a big batch of apple butter after school tomorrow, and I need a couple strong men to help me. Do you know of anyone who might be available?"

The boys looked at each other, then at Vern. "I don't know," Harland said. "Maybe."

"Maybe, huh? You got plans?" Della asked.

Harland glanced at Vern again. Vern winked.

wwnw

Della noticed that Vern slept strangely well that night, nary a toss or turn. He didn't exercise enough during the day, so he usually thrashed under the covers at night. When he entered the kitchen the next morning, Della asked if he'd like some coffee. He said yes, thank you, after he woke up the boys. He smiled. He never smiled or offered to wake up the boys. Lately, he didn't rise before the boys left for school.

Della could hear Harland and Mylan giggling in their room. Vern's voice sounded deep and muddled. He talked for a long time. She suspected they were planning some fun she would object to—a trip to the go-kart track, or a demolition derby, maybe.

All three of them ran into the kitchen. The boys smiled up at her like they had a secret they were dying to spill. Vern said, "Now, we can't jump the gun. Lady of the house has final say." Della passed bacon and eggs and ketchup and leftover fried chicken—just a few thighs and drumsticks.

Plate filled, Vern turned to Della. He said, "I'm gonna dig a moat all around this property. 'Cause my house is my castle, and you are my queen. I won't stop with this moat, though. You know how we've always talked about starting our own business?"

"A moat? Like medieval times? Why would anyone want that in their yard?" Had this terrible idea been spiraling in his brain while he'd rested so meekly last night? She wanted to laugh but he looked so serious. Besides, they already had Della's Delectables.

"Vern's Moats, we'll call it. I'll take commissions from people who want moats around their own yards. We'll excavate one here first to let everybody see what we can do. It'll be a show moat. We'll put some signs on the highway: 'Come see the Show Moat, and find out how to get your own.'"

Demand would be huge, he told her, especially around Valentine's Day, though the frozen ground might present excavation problems. He already knew the basics from his time at the quarry. He even had plans for minimoats for doghouses. He figured everyone in Saline

County would be clamoring for a moat for aesthetic and security reasons. "They're romantic, too, as I said about the queen stuff. A moat fit for a queen in her castle. We could sell lawn ornaments that look like crocodiles or moat monsters. Moat ornaments, I guess they'd be."

"My," Della said. Her family studied her face.

"I knew she wouldn't like it, boys," Vern snapped. "She can have her own business but God forbid anyone else tries to do something for this family." The boys turned their eyes to the floor. Mylan sighed hard.

"I didn't mean I didn't like it," Della said, half for the boys, half for how the project might give Vern something to do so he wasn't underfoot and paranoid. He hadn't stopped perusing the crime blotter. "Maybe this would be just the thing. You and the boys could work on the ditch together."

Vern had risen half out of his seat still grasping a chicken leg, his shoulders tense. Now he settled back, picked the bone clean with his teeth, and tossed it on the plate. "It's not a ditch. It's a moat," he grumbled.

Harland asked, "Are you going to use C-4 to make the moat?"

"Nah, son, we aren't digging down but ten feet or so. Not as far as the substrate. Though if we did, we'd have no need for the garden hose for water. Eventually, we'd hit the water table, and the thing would fill up like a big old well. Wouldn't that be something?"

"I'm sure you know what you're doing," Della said. Vern was moving way too fast. He'd trapped her using the boys as bait.

"Yep, the only thing I regret is that the moat won't be done in time for an anniversary present. June 2! Bet you thought I'd forgotten." Vern kicked back in his chair and scratched his belly.

wmm

During the next week, from what Della could tell from the kitchen, moat planning involved Vern getting drunk. He'd drain a six-pack of High Life and pace the yard with new clarity, his bandy legs lifting higher than they needed to with each step.

He'd sprint inside panting, grab Della, and tell her things. Once he said that he saw the problem with his plot of land, and with Kansas in general: "The ground is too level around the house. There's no trees to speak of. Everybody who takes half a glance from the road can see our whole spread crystal clear."

"I don't know why that's such a problem," Della said.

"But what if you're out front tending the garden, all bent over in your shorts, them riding up your legs, and some pervert spots you."

"I don't find that very likely, Vern. Only four or five cars pass on any given day."

"It only takes one," Vern said, low and foreboding, yet still smiling. "One to park a half mile up the road and sneak back after dark with a big knife, and rape you and make the boys watch and slice their throats, all before I had the chance to fight back."

"Nobody'd rape or slice you, though, huh?"

"Nope," Vern said.

One night Della sat down beside Vern on the couch and told him how Harland and Mylan were outgrowing their clothes. Harland couldn't bend his elbows in his dress shirt, it stretched so tight on his back, and Mylan's elastic-waist shorts cut into his belly skin.

"We need money, Vern, to buy the boys things," Della said. "And my jam can only do so much."

Vern said, "You remember Perry at that Mobil station on Crawford? He told me a while ago that they needed more guys. In a week or two, I'll talk to him. Just till I get the moats going, though. That's the real plan." He sighed, hitched his pants up, and pulled her down onto his lap. His belt buckle dug into her side. She was glad he was laying off the moat. Maybe he'd forget entirely, like he had the nightcrawler business or the sub sandwich shop a few years ago. Each time they drove past the Captain Nemo's franchise on Iron Street, Vern would pine for what might have been.

"Whose wife are you, sweetheart?" Vern asked now.

"Yours, honey."

"Mine and only mine?"

"Yes. Yours and only yours." They had played this game when they first got married, when words like "wife," "husband," and "our flatware pattern" still sounded exciting, when Della was still caught up in that intermingled grief at losing her father and delight at finding Vern—so strong, so handsome.

He kissed her and slid his square hand along the waistband of her sweatpants. When he started fumbling with the drawstring, Della's mind raced for an excuse. He had become so amorous lately. He used to get home from the quarry too exhausted to think about anything except soaking up TV and a High Life. Now, he said he was "ready to eat a piece of you, you look so tasty."

Vern held her with his fingers laced around her back.

She had a double batch of blueberry bubbling on the stove, and she could just picture it boiling over on her white Formica countertop. Those stains would be a bear to scrub away. She slid away onto her feet.

"Don't be a tease," Vern said. He let her go and patted her rump as she retreated to her kitchen.

✻✻✻✻

Over the next few weeks, between batches of jam, Della watched Vern and the boys from the kitchen window. Vern would bring a load of limestone from the quarry, the truck riding low with the weight of the smooth, buff-colored slabs. He still had a friend who got him free off-cuts.

School ended in late May, so Vern and the boys spent whole days outside. They used shovels to dig a trench around the perimeter of the manicured grass. Della couldn't invite her friends and neighbors over because Vern and the boys had created such an eyesore, but then again, friends and neighbors had rarely visited before. The family didn't exactly live on the main drag. Their house wasn't the sort of place where people just popped in. Unless they were perverts, if Vern were correct. Which he wasn't.

One day, Vern rumbled up in a backhoe. Della prayed it was just rented. Grinding gears accompanied Della's jam making for the next few days, and the moat hole grew much quicker. Dust from the excavation blew through the cracks in the windows, and she had to be vigilant to keep the particles from tainting her batches.

A couple days after the heavy equipment arrived, Della picked the first strawberries of the summer from her little garden plot and stowed them in her apron. She glanced at the construction. Vern and Harland were standing around in hard hats while the backhoe bit chunks out of their yard. But if Vern was not operating the backhoe, who was? Della ran to them, shielding her eyes from the sun as she looked up and saw Mylan's head, barely poking up over the steering wheel.

"Why is Mylan running the backhoe?" she asked.

Vern said, "Settle down now, Della, Mylan's plenty old enough to run a backhoe. You should be proud of him, the way he handles that double clutch." The bucket paused at the top of its arc like a beckoning finger.

"Come down, baby," Della called. She could only raise one arm to Mylan—the other held the berries in her apron. "Nice and slow." She almost grasped his foot.

Mylan shook his head. "No way, Warty," he yelled. He kicked her hand away. Lately, Vern called her "Little Mrs. Worrywart." Mylan and Harland picked it up and started calling her Worrywart or Ms. Wart or just Warty.

"Hey now," Vern said.

Mylan straightened right up.

"Apologize to your mother."

"I'm sorry," Mylan said, not looking at Della. "Do I have to get off?" he asked Vern.

"Nah, that's okay, son."

Mylan and Harland seemed to have forgotten all about how Vern would rip limbs off action figures that weren't stored as he'd asked, how Della was the one who cuddled them and told them Vern didn't mean anything by it, he just had a temper.

"You go on back into your kitchen now," Vern said.

Della slunk to the house, closing the door on Vern yelling, "Woo-boy, son! Get it." She could just imagine that Mylan'd get the gearshift confused and bring that heavy shovel part down on his brother's head. Then she had an evil thought: if Mylan dropped the shovel on Vern's head, they could bury him in the moat and pretend he'd never happened.

When she opened her apron, the strawberries were smashed into the cloth. She rinsed the berries in her colander and threw them in her pot, her hands trembling.

uMMm

A few days later, Della asked if she could take the truck for the jam delivery because she hadn't been to town in such a long time. For the past month, Vern had been running her jams into town and picking up new supplies, and she missed her chats with Crystal. In fact, she realized she hadn't seen anybody but Vern and the boys for weeks.

Vern said, "I'm using limestone rather than brick to edge the moat. Limestone is craggier than brick. Lots of people don't think about that. It affects the way you mix the concrete. My mix is smoother."

"Honey, you didn't hear me. Could I have the truck for an hour or so?"

"The truck? Nah, I don't think so." Vern waved her away.

Della waited for his explanation, but it never came.

"The truck, Vern. I'm taking it."

"I don't think so," Vern said. "The carburetor's been real funny on that truck, and I'm the only one who knows how to tweak it."

"Sometimes I get the feeling you don't want me to leave the house."

"Now why would you think that? Though the boys and I do miss you terribly when you're gone. You're the heart of our home, Della."

The heart. Della liked that.

uMMm

26

The next day, an etched limestone sign appeared in the yard. "For Della," it said. Vern told her, "Del, this moat is like my Taj Mahal, just for you."

Della asked, "Wasn't the wife of the man who built the Taj Mahal dead?"

"Yep," Vern replied. He pointed out how there was room at the top of the plaque for more engraving, and that "In Memoriam" could be added easily, along with applicable dates, God forbid.

Vern cut their home phone service. He explained that because of moat cost overruns, they couldn't afford a regular phone anymore. He had gotten a prepaid cell, though, which he kept on his belt loop. He told her just let him know whenever she wanted to call anyone. She once asked him if she could borrow the cell phone to call Crystal, but he said he was waiting for an important business call, and besides, his device was out of batteries. He and the boys communicated across the yard using walkie-talkies. The boys thought it was funny to make farting noises into the walkie-talkie and yell, "Excuse me!" Della thought it was kind of funny, too, but Vern didn't. He said they should respect their equipment.

Something strange was happening with Crystal. Vern brought back less and less money from the jam. There was only twenty-five dollars from the last batch. This made no sense, because Della always asked Vern how many jars Crystal wanted, and he always said, "Same as last week." What was she doing with all that extra jam, if she wasn't selling it?

She'd asked Vern about the jam. He told her something about Crystal doing a new mail-order business so she needed a bigger inventory. It hadn't made a lot of sense.

Vern poured the floor of the moat in mid-June. Once the concrete dried, Vern built up the inner walls using limestone chunks. He told his sons, "Men, we're protecting the house from bad guys. Make these walls real thick, okay. Nobody's going to sneak in and get your mother." The boys hopped up and down in their little tan steel-toed boots and added extra smears of concrete with their child-size trowels.

Neither of them kissed their mother goodnight anymore. They ducked their heads and pretended to be asleep when she went to tuck them in. Probably just a phase. They'd been mama's boys for so long that it was high time Vern got a turn.

wwww

On July Fourth, the moat was ready. Vern decided a ceremony was in order. He and the boys wore their suits, and Vern insisted that Della put on a nice dress. Harland played the trumpet with the school band. He could toot out taps or "Twinkle, Twinkle, Little Star," so Vern chose taps because it better matched the gravity of the occasion. Vern ran a large-nozzled pump and hose from their well over to the empty moat and sent Mylan around with a monkey wrench to make sure the couplings were tight. As Harland sputtered away on trumpet, Vern opened a spigot, and the first rush of water splashed the moat floor. The family watched the puddle spread and soak the concrete until it became clear that the moat would not appear before their very eyes. The trench took a week to fill.

wwww

Just as the water finally lapped the top edge of the limestone, Della tried sneaking past Vern with her boxes of jam. She was nervous, though she'd told herself it would just be a fun surprise for Vern when she got back. Save him a trip. She looked over her shoulder as she got the jam all loaded in the truck. As she slid the keys into the ignition, Vern appeared at the driver's side window. Della jumped. Vern peered into the cab, his eyes moving over every inch of her and the upholstery.

"Vern," Della said, putting a hand over her chest to conceal the pounding of her heart. "I was thinking I'd take the truck out for a little spin, go on down to the store. I'm getting stir-crazy in this place."

After a long pause, Vern said, "You said you were headed out with the jam? Tell you what, let me take it for you. I'm going to town anyway to get an estimate on some ten-foot pikes." He opened the truck door.

Della stayed a moment, her fingers clasping the steering wheel. Vern lifted her hands away and set them in her lap. He slid her across the vinyl seat and out, onto the road. "Easy, there," he told her.

When Vern returned with the pikes (the estimate must have been reasonable), it was twilight. Della had been sitting on the porch swing for several hours, gazing at the moat. She had a terrible feeling that if she didn't get away now, she never would, and the boys wouldn't either. An image came to her, one she'd call up often in times of difficulty. She lay on her deathbed. A rustic quilt covered her. Her heavily tendoned, liver-spotted hands lay limp in her sons' hands, Harland's hard from working the land, and Mylan's soft from his study of business, the knowledge he'd gained at college turning Della and him into a real Ms. and Mr. Smuckers. "We love you, Mother," the boys would croon in reedy harmony, as she drifted toward eternal repose. And where was Vern? Vern was ever absent, dead and buried somewhere, or not. Blown to bits, most likely, and scattered through the quarry—a bloody stump, a dab of viscera, a spatter of blood over the rock. But Vern had bucked that plan. He looked to be the survivor in the current scenario.

Vern was going to walk straight past her into the house, but Della grabbed the edge of his T-shirt. She asked, "Why aren't you showing the moat to anyone yet, now that it's done?"

Vern sat down on the swing beside her, draping an arm across the back of her neck. "I don't really want to bring loads of people over here to see it. That would defeat the whole purpose."

"I thought the purpose was making some money."

"Honey. The world's too dangerous for us to go out there and deal with people like that. To engage promiscuously in commerce. You're staying right here with me forever, okay?" He stroked her cheek with the backs of his sandpapery fingers. Della rose, went inside, and shut the door. Nothing bad was happening here. Not in her little house. She just had to keep her wits about her. The way bad things worked was they snuck up on you. One false step on a quarry ledge, just when your footing felt sure.

wwwn

The next day dawned clear and cool. Della opened the kitchen window to pick up the breeze. The moat wasn't looking so bad now that the heavy equipment was gone. Vern set the limestone perfectly level, she could say that for him. Maybe she and the boys could get a fossil guidebook and try to identify the creatures that had died in the limestone centuries ago, when the whole state of Kansas was covered by an ocean. A moat was just a tiny little thing, relatively speaking. A drop in the bucket.

Or they could have a big party for her upcoming birthday. Show Crystal and her husband and the boys' friends the monstrosity. She overheard Harland and Vern standing in the shade of the house talking. Harland said, "Dad, Crystal came by again. I told her Mom wasn't home."

"Good job, son. It's important we keep the outsiders away."

Della stepped back from the window, feeling cold despite the kitchen's heat. After ten minutes, she nearly had herself convinced that the conversation she'd overheard never happened. What she had really heard was that Harland had called Crystal on the telephone, but she wasn't home. They were probably planning a surprise party for her birthday, and of course Crystal would be invited. Also, a finger of land wide enough to drive the truck across remained. The moat was not yet impregnable. She told herself these things and didn't quite believe them.

When Vern came in for lunch, she asked him, "What's up with that one little spit of land on the moat?" Her voice was even. Vern didn't know she knew about Crystal. She'd been hiding her emotions from Vern for so long that it was no challenge now.

"Oh, right beside the guard tower? That's where the drawbridge will go, honey. Yep, that will be gone by tomorrow. We're going to get the bulldozer back and knock it right down. We've finally got all the supplies collected on this side of the moat, so we don't need an easy way across anymore. There'll be a password for the drawbridge," he added.

"Oh, that's fun. Do I get to help choose?"

Vern looked away for a moment, his face pained, and said, "The boys and I talked about this, Del, and we've decided that it's best if you don't know it. You're our weak link, physically, and someone could, God forbid, use force to get it from you. It would compromise the integrity of our compound." Della thought about arguing with him. She could point out that though she was a woman, surely she would fare better in a fight than her eight-year-old son. But she knew such an argument would hold no water with Vern. Her father told her a wise woman picked her battles.

Della discovered her unsold jam when she went to look for empty jars in the garage. Boxes stacked on boxes, the bright pink of the strawberry, the deep magenta of the mulberry, the cerise of the rose hip, all her work, weeks of it, there in one place. It was awe-inspiring, really, how much she'd done, and she gave herself a moment to appreciate it. The boxes were stacked roughly, and a peach batch had broken on the concrete. Wasps buzzed the sharded jars, their flight paths crazy, their wings slow from the sugar.

wwww

Della lay sleepless beside Vern that night. When had he gone around the bend, sanitywise? Where had he even learned about things like the "integrity of the compound"? She and the boys would be trapped tomorrow. She struggled and struggled, but she kept coming back to one conclusion—the only conclusion: she couldn't be in that house come morning, and neither could the boys. She would spirit her children away, and then, she and Vern could sort everything out once they'd all gotten some distance, physically and emotionally. And by sort she meant divorce. Obviously, she couldn't get any distance while she was surrounded by the moat.

Della tried three times to get out of bed. Each time she eased herself upright, she heard Vern stir, so she settled back on the mattress, making sure that her breathing was slow and regular. On her fourth try, Vern didn't move a muscle.

She crept to Vern's side of the bed, grabbed his keys from the night table, and ran over the carpet on bare feet, her nightgown flapping her thighs. She scooped Mylan out of bed but found Harland's bed empty.

She dashed through the house carrying Mylan, searching each room for her lost boy. She went outside, but he wasn't there, either. Finally, she shook Mylan gently and asked him, "Where's your brother, honey? Where's Harland?"

"In the guard tower," he mumbled.

Vern and the boys had built the guard tower the previous week. It was fifteen feet tall with a roofed hut on top. Sure enough, Harland peered down. He wore camouflage hunting pants and held an air rifle.

Della called through ragged breaths, "Come on, honey. We're going to get on out of here for a while. Just you boys and me. A real trip."

Harland stepped away from the railing. He returned with a walkie-talkie. "Daddy said you might try this," he told her. He spoke into the walkie-talkie, "Big Eagle, Big Eagle, come in. This is Little Eagle One. She's trying to get away."

There was a long pause. Then the crackling reply, "I'll be right out, soldier." As Della gazed up at Harland, she loosened her grip on Mylan. He wriggled away and climbed to his brother.

She yelled up, "Come on guys. We can get ice cream. You don't want me to go without you, do you?" She took a half step toward the truck.

They looked down at her, their faces hard to read.

"Please, honey? Mylan? Last one to the pickup's a rotten egg."

Mylan chewed his fingers and Harland played with the walkie-talkie. Della scanned the yard for Vern. Still no sign.

"Hey there, boys, I'll take you to the Walmart. It's open twenty-four hours. You can have as many toys as you can carry. What do you say?"

Harland set his air rifle on the railing and brought his eye to the sight.

"Now, Harland, you stop that right now," Della yelled. Harland pulled the trigger. The shot hit the dust at Della's feet.

A second shot whistled by her head. Della ran for the truck. She threw open the door and hopped in. Vern had the seat adjusted for his longer legs, and Della didn't have time to fix it. She pulled her weight down onto the clutch and brake, using the steering wheel for leverage. She heard more shots, but she didn't turn to see how close they were. Tears blurred her vision.

She jammed the key into the ignition and made the motor roar. She did some split-second bargaining—she could retrieve the kids tomorrow morning. Or better yet, she decided as she punched the accelerator, she'd come back for them, later that night, with friends for backup. Crystal and her husband would help. The important part was that someone got out right now.

But as Della sped along their gravel driveway toward the hunk of land connecting their family to the rest of the world, Mylan stepped smack-dab in its center, blocking her way. He waved his arms, yelling for her to stop. She was going too fast.

She swerved to avoid hitting him, and the truck went into a skid. During the moment she spun out, she saw the moat come close, its dark water. A white flash of Mylan's pajamas as the truck's wheels slid off the edge of the land. A racing engine. Tires spinning. Her head banged the steering wheel. Warm blood stung her eyes. Cold water sopped her feet. No sense of up or down, forward or back, home-side or world-side. Her wrist throbbed. The front end of the truck pitched forward from the weight of the engine and the water held the doors shut. A shrill cry erupted from her mouth. When she closed her mouth, a thick, hollow silence settled in. The slurp of water filled the cab. The fog on the windows from her hot, fast breath. The water enveloped her calves, tickled her thighs, and lapped up her stomach. It was telling her something. What was it saying? None of us gets final say. Her head felt so heavy that she set it on the steering wheel.

The water licked her chin, and she remembered her wedding day, Vern's hand cold as he tilted her chin up for their wedded kiss.

The church was all blank, high ceilings—stark as the quarry. As bride and groom left the church through the waiting crowd, a gunshot cut across the happy voices. Vern had plied three of his cousins, in town for the weekend from Culvert, with a thirty-pack of High Life to give him and his bride a three-gun salute. One of the boys had an itchy trigger finger. He shot early. A startled flock of crows rose croaking from an ancient cottonwood. The other cousins shot and shot and shot into the sky.

A crow hit her ten-year-old flower girl on the shoulder, where it stuck. The girl shook her arms and screamed, but the bird remained. Della rushed forward and knocked the bird off with her bridal bouquet. The crow hit the ground, a ruffled mass of feathers. Blood dripped from the lilies of the valley in her bouquet. "Look at what your idiot cousins did," she said to Vern.

"That bird shouldn't have flown in front of the boys' guns," Vern had told her. "What did it think would happen?"

The Tunnel

MIRIAM DELIVERED A SPEECH over the intercom. The title: "Miriam Will Fulfill All of Your Fantasies." She'd written and edited it for a week during her classes, highlighting the words she wanted to emphasize in gold sparkly ink and the regular old words in purple sparkly ink. The gold sparkly ink was hard to read. Her voice quavered a little on the first line, "My name is Miriam Green. I'm a seventh grader and I'm running for student council president," but then her words grew surer. With great conviction, she promised pop machines and early dismissals. Miriam had to lean sideways to get to the microphone because the vice principal crouched beside her with his finger poised on the off button. He had damp circles in his pits and smelled like a weird mix of Pine-Sol and old cigarettes. There'd been teacher resignations and a couple suicides (eighth-grade American history, reading), and the vice principal had to cover a lot of classes. Outside his office, a long line of students waited to be disciplined.

When she finished, the vice principal said, "Well done, Miriam," within hearing range of her loitering classmates. They wore T-shirts with the arms cut off, windows to their chests and nipples, their pale biceps marked by cigarette burns and tattoos of happy faces and knives. During art class, Miriam had watched a couple of boys doing a tattoo of a snake, stabbing with a sewing needle, popped Bic pens for ink. At one point she asked, "Wouldn't you rather use black ink? Blue's just gonna look like a bruise." The tattooer had asked if she wanted him to tattoo her face, so she stopped talking.

The other candidate for student council president, Glen Hopley, had given his speech the previous morning. He yelled, "Fuckfuckfuckfuck-fuck," until they pulled the plug. That was the reason the vice principal now rode the off button with such gusto. Miriam was disappointed the administrators let her speak. If they hadn't, she could've said that was the reason she didn't win, when she didn't win, which she wouldn't. It was so dumb. Glen got nominated as a joke, while her candidacy was serious business. Good grades, volunteer work, leadership positions in extracurriculars. Single cobblestones paving her way out of Kansas. Last semester in biology, Glen had eaten an earthworm he should have dissected. He always did things like that. Everybody loved him. She wondered if he knew that formaldehyde was a carcinogen.

The wild part was she and Glen had plenty in common: they were both as romantically repulsive as the vice principal's pit stains, Glen because he was literally grotesque, Miriam for complicated reasons. Such a little achiever. She tried not to let on how good her grades were, but the teachers used her as an example in class. And she had to do de-meaning things like cheat on the push-up test in gym to get her A. And pretend she didn't have a huge vocabulary, and intentionally violate rules of subject-verb agreement in conversation with her peers. As if poor grammar might make them like her or want to date her. It didn't matter what these kids thought. Though she didn't hate the other kids. She wanted to make out with them, but she wouldn't because making out was a slippery slope to unplanned pregnancy to no access to abortions to birthing a disgusting noisy baby to dropping out to getting your neighbor to babysit so you can work the lunch shift at Applebee's for forty dollars a shot and you learn much too late your neighbor is a molester and that's why he wanted to babysit. Then you have to repair unfixable damage to the psyche of your poor child, who never asked to be born. All that time the father is absent due to the demands of his amateur dirt bike career. Applebee's won't even give you free lunch, just a discount. It's no kind of life.

wwww

Miriam left the office, hall pass in hand. Just outside stood the rearing mustang that, a plaque read, a shop student named Fred Armstrong had carved from a cottonwood stump nearly fifty years ago, in 1952. The mascot stood only three feet tall, more like a foal. A pedestal brought it to eye level. The mustang was presented to Roosevelt-Lincoln Middle School, the plaque continued, in appreciation of the solid foundation the institution bestowed upon everyone who passed through its doors, readying them for bigger and better things, like high school. Over the years, pocketknives had excised the mustang's eyes. Its flank bore a swastika; its legs were shaved down to sticks.

Fred Armstrong was the sort of student Miriam wanted to be, remembered long after he was gone. But he was a boy and handy with a chainsaw. Probably everyone loved dear Fred. They grasped where he came from because they came from there too.

Miriam always fell a little short. Her name, even, was too long and weird. She'd looked it up in a baby name book at the mall and found it meant "sea of sorrows." That sounded about right. Her father said it meant "mistress of the sea." Maybe he had consulted a different baby name book. Miriam trusted the book in the mall.

Miriam knew she could find a place where she and her name weren't weird, where being a smart woman wasn't a double bind. These places existed on TV. If the first place she tried was no good, she'd go somewhere else. Basically, she had to not get pregnant. Leverage her academic success to a one-way trip out of town. Could she win an election if she weren't popular? Maybe she was popular, though, in the same way everyone in town liked the Chinese buffet. The battered fried meat balanced out the unfamiliar sauces. Miriam worried there was nothing to balance her out. But she'd pandered in her speech. Reached her five-spice chicken wing across the aisle.

To get to home economics class, she had to descend to the bottom floor of Roosevelt Building, drop again into a tunnel, and rise into Lincoln. The time she left the office had not been noted on her pass, so she dawdled. The hallway in Roosevelt was painted with a jungle mural. Someone had Sharpied in anatomically correct (male, human) reproductive organs on the giraffes' and tigers' and monkeys' nether regions. Maybe once she was president, she could engage a team to restore the mural, along with Fred's horse.

She stopped for drinks at each fountain and visited each restroom. She stared at her reflection in each mirror, turning her head to find her best angle, which was chin down, three-quarter right profile. Her left eye tended to get a little squinty, especially when she smiled. She washed her hands in each restroom sink. A few times she washed them twice. Sometimes she washed her hands fifteen times a day, and other times twenty. She spread Vaseline on her hands every night and pulled tube socks over them so her sheets wouldn't get greasy, but still her hands cracked and reddened.

When Miriam reached the tunnel between Roosevelt and Lincoln, she stayed toward the center and walked fast. Junk built up along the walls: Laffy Taffy wrappers, fake gold chains, hair elastics, pizza crusts, limp condoms. The wet air smelled of sweat and yeast and weed and cigarettes and something darker and stranger. The closest thing she could compare it to was a shiitake mushroom grow kit her mother had gotten her for Christmas. No one had realized you needed to open the kit immediately, so it sat wrapped among all the other presents until it leaked evil brown liquid over the tree skirt.

Weak light bulbs flickered in wire cages overhead. The walls sweated oil that had evaporated off students' bodies. If you rubbed against the walls, you came away with a yellow smear on your sleeve. For just a second, Miriam wanted to lick the walls.

She caught sight of a wadded pink "Miriam Will Fulfill All of Your Fantasies" campaign poster toward the middle of the tunnel. She uncurled it with her foot. A handwritten addendum read: "for $20 a Nite."

Maybe if she were president she'd do nothing at all except try to make some friends. Her friends from elementary school had become obsessed with a boy band. They each had their own boy whom they loved, and there were only five boys, and Miriam was the sixth girl. Why wasn't one of the other friends the sixth girl? Even if there had been a boy available, Miriam didn't think she'd be interested. What was the point? They'd never meet Brayden or Jaxon or Slade in real life.

Miriam had a dream once about one perfect boy, who had dark hair and skin and who was only a little taller than her, whose curly hair was so soft when she touched it. In her dream, they were together on a very small island, lying together in the sand. He had a penis that unrolled like a cartoon tongue, down his leg and across to hers. It crept up her thigh. She liked it. That's when she woke up. She didn't like thinking about the dream but did nearly every day. She was thinking about it right now.

She thought about something else: after she won this election, she'd be all set to become freshman class president next year, when her résumé started to count. She wouldn't have to do much student governing this year, just give a few speeches. Let R-L follow its natural course toward decay and ruin, like all things.

The school's brick facade looked solid. Maybe stern and forbidding, if anything. It wasn't until you stepped inside that you noticed the gum stuck to doorknobs, jammed in locker vents, and ground into carpeting, the roofs leaking yellow liquid that the janitors caught in trash barrels in the halls. The ceilings, it was rumored, sloughed pure asbestos. Particles floated down to the scarred desks. Students brushed the dust to the floor each morning with the heels of their hands. College admissions officers evaluating her résumé wouldn't know what it meant to be president of a place like this. They'd picture it like the outside, all trim and upstanding. She wouldn't disabuse them of that fantasy.

wmm

All the other students turned toward her when she entered home ec. The room, with its kitchenette units ringing a group of tables and chairs, smelled of cheap beef and oven cleaner. Nobody said anything about her speech, which made her sad and glad in equal measure.

Ms. Pygott made Miriam be partners with Manny, who was left over. She knew why.

Last class, a couple boys had gotten to school early and spent a good twenty minutes spitting on Miriam's assigned seat. She'd seen the glisten of saliva just a second before she lowered herself. She sat on the edge of a table, unsure. Everyone stared and whispered. The spitters hid their smiles behind their hands. She wasn't sure if they had chosen her seat randomly, or because they liked her, or because they didn't.

Manny Rodriguez, a kid with a round head and dark hair who always walked around smiling so you started to wonder if maybe he was slow, had grabbed Miriam's arm to stop her from sitting. Then, he wiped the saliva off her chair with the sleeve of his plaid work shirt. The spit soaked the red and black fabric. He nodded toward the chair, so she sat down. It was dry, but she'd never wear that skirt again. What a gentlemanly gesture—so rare, so wasteful. Each kitchenette was stocked with paper towels. The guys who'd spit on the chair stared at her and Manny the rest of the class. Miriam practically ran when the bell rang.

Today, Ms. Pygott explained, the class would make Orange Juliuses and donuts. Ms. Pygott assigned each cooking pair a kitchenette and showed them how to use the blender and deep fryer. "This is a Fry Baby," she told Miriam and Manny. "It's the smaller size. When you set up your household, you're going to want a larger model, with a deep oil reservoir. We've got the FryDaddy at my house. It's big enough even for chicken fried steaks."

Miriam nodded slightly and did a tight-lipped smile. Lack of response made Ms. Pygott leave quicker. Ms. Pygott finally moved on to the next kitchenette.

"Do you want to do the donuts or the Juliuses?" Miriam asked Manny.

"Juliuses, I guess," Manny said. "I liked your speech. I'll vote for you, for sure."

"Thanks." Miriam pretended to sift the flour for Ms. Pygott's benefit, dumped it into a bowl, and added the sugar and egg. Then she stopped.

One kitchenette over, a tall boy with the white-blond hair you saw only on the children who lived far out in the country was glaring at them.

"Is that one of the guys who spit on my chair?" she asked Manny.

"Yep," he said. "That's Mylan. He's never liked me anyway."

"Why not?" Miriam asked.

Manny shrugged. "He told me to go back to Mexico once. Maybe that's it."

"I'm sorry," Miriam said.

Manny cleaned their blender jar by squirting some dishwashing solution in and rubbing vigorously with his hands. He didn't wash his hands first, and even if he had, it wouldn't matter. His hands were covered in warts. Not like three or four. More like twenty-six. Per hand. Could she catch warts? Miriam imagined her digestive track filled with red lesions that wept each time she swallowed. That would be a problem.

Ms. Pygott always forced them to eat everything they cooked. The Julius was liquid, every bit of it contaminated by those hands. Miriam dropped a glob of batter into the Fry Baby and watched it pop. The blender roared behind her. It was nearly Julius time. Miriam prayed the school's wiring might finally give out and short-circuit the blender. But no. Manny set a Julius in front of her.

She told Manny, "I'm not drinking any calories this week. You can have two if you want." She watched his hands on the icy cup for a second too long.

"They're not contagious," he said. He was still smiling at her, even after he'd noticed that she found his hands gross. Why was he still smiling at her?

"I know," Miriam said. She pulled the donut out of the fryer and dumped it on a paper towel, which turned translucent as it absorbed oil.

"Okay," he said, eyeing the donut.

"Do you want my donut, too?" She pushed it toward him. It was the least she could do. He ate the donut in one bite and used the greasy paper towel to dab his lips. She imagined kissing Manny. He could wear gloves and grab her waist. Pick her up so she could wrap her legs around him. His hair was shiny. His lips looked soft. A magazine said use a homemade sugar scrub to exfoliate your lips before kissing. It said the best sex position for the woman was on top, facing the partner. The best sex position for the man was the woman on top, backward, which was called the reverse cowgirl. Also, men liked the pile driver, where you put your legs over your head and they stood while they penetrated you. It also said you could have sex on the beach in public if the man sat in a beach chair, a towel spread over your lap for modesty. Watch out for sand, it warned.

Miriam and Manny cleaned their work area. The bell rang and everyone left except Ms. Pygott, who was checking on all the Fry Babies.

wWmw

Over the next week, R-L fell apart faster than usual, or maybe Miriam just paid more attention. The tunnel accreted congealed oil like earwax. Mechanical pencils were thrust up the mustang's nose, where they dangled like tusks. A canister of pepper spray exploded in someone's locker, and everyone wept and coughed in the band hallway. Tennis shoes with their laces knotted were tossed in the gym rafters. The janitors forgot to change the trash barrels catching the roof leaks over a stormy weekend, and the containers overflowed. Rainwater soaked the wooden joists and plaster of the upper floor of Roosevelt. One day, a girl put her foot through a third-floor hallway, and the milling kids on the second floor didn't notice the foot dangling from the ceiling until her flip-flop fell on someone's head. The janitors marched around with mops and cones and construction tape. The girl said her parents were going to sue the school.

During kickball in PE, Glen Hopley got a home run and crawled the bases grunting like a pig. There was no grass outside R-L, only asphalt, so he rubbed his knees and palms raw. He charged a group of girls and threatened to bleed on them. They scattered laughing. Miriam flied out to the pitcher. The gym teacher watched all the girls emerge naked from the shower in their towels, checking them off on her clipboard.

Miriam started talking to some new girls at lunch, and they told her that she should look for a guy with a small penis to have sex with, because it wouldn't hurt so bad. They gave her a few names. One of the girls opened her binder to reveal a series of pencil lines, named and annotated: Jacob P. 4.5", Mylan 6.25", Little Ben 7.5". She was flunking math but had a head for some numbers. Little Ben was only five feet tall!

Miriam got to school early each morning to put up more campaign posters. Once, when she was struggling to get the tape to stick to the tunnel wall, she saw a moving shadow at the far end. She yelled, "Hey," and the shadow melted away. She wondered if it might have been Glen. Another time after school Miriam found a Mike and Ike with the top layer licked off stuck in her hair. She washed her hair three times in a row and still it didn't feel clean. In home ec they made sloppy joes. They made bierocks. They made Mexican pizzas, which had corn.

One day, Ms. Pygott woke the Fry Babies, and the class cooked corn dogs. Manny was her partner again. That blond boy Mylan still lurked and watched. Miriam wondered if he was the Mylan from the girl's measurement list. Surely there weren't multiple Mylans. Manny ate both their corndogs without even asking. He bolted out the door after class, leaving Miriam with the ketchup-smeared dishes. Once she got them washed, she had to hurry down Lincoln's stairs, through the tunnel, and up another set of stairs in Roosevelt to her English class. She was making great time when she got stuck in a crowd at the tunnel mouth. The bodies all pressed together reminded her of elementary school, when she and her friends had clogged the tunnel slide. One person would slide down to the bottom and wedge his legs against the roof, everyone stacked like Pringles, the air warmed from their shared breath. Their voices were muffled by their coats and scarves.

One time on the slide, it wasn't fun. She could feel sneakers in her back. The feet pushed harder and harder, and still the slide remained corked. The air was all used up. She kicked the head of the boy below her. He yelped, and soon, she sprawled gasping in the light, her nose shoved into dusty wood chips.

That same panic gripped her now. She could have lifted her feet and remained upright, the bodies were packed so tight. Only one thing could draw such a crowd, and sure enough, the cries came, "Fight! Fight! Fight!" Then, as always, the students all fell silent. The air tingled with expectation as everyone strained to see.

Through a halo of empty space, Miriam spotted two boys by a wall with arms locked around each other's necks, punching and pulling ears, biting hair, slamming elbows into stomachs.

The tall blond boy was winning. He grabbed the shorter kid by the neck and slammed the top of his head into the tunnel wall. Once. Twice. Three times. Blood streaked the wall. She stood on her tiptoes to look for warts on the shorter one and hoped to see none. He raised a hand to his bloody face and she saw the warts. Manny.

Miriam tried to push through the crowd, but she was pinned. Manny's head met the wall one last time, and the tall boy dropped him. Manny slumped, a pile of limbs.

The vice principal pushed through. Kids yelled warnings, and those at the outside of the crowd melted away. The blond boy bounded down the tunnel into Roosevelt. "Stop him!" the vice principal shouted. The students cleared a path. The vice principal kneeled by Manny.

Now everyone headed to class. The halls again hummed with retellings of the fight for those who missed it or had a poor view. Miriam got stuck in a corner. She didn't want to take her eyes off Manny, as though her gaze might heal him. A couple times, she thought she saw Manny's chest rise and fall. The vice principal rubbed Manny's chest and spoke quietly. She waited long past the other students cleared away. She waited long past the bell. The tunnel was very quiet now, almost peaceful. She stepped off the stairs. The sound made the vice principal turn.

"Is he okay?" she asked.

"Get to class," the vice principal yelled.

Miriam ran past him and out the mouth of the tunnel. The bright lights in Roosevelt's hallway made her squint. She heard sirens getting louder as she passed the zoo mural. Someone had added a long swoop of jizz to the toucan phallus since she'd seen it last. The monkey caught the milky strand in his mouth.

On the landing between the second and third floors she found him blocking her way, the white-haired boy who'd beat her friend. He paced, though the space was so tight he could only manage two steps each way before he had to turn.

She dropped her backpack. He jumped. "I thought you were the vice principal," he said. He smiled, revealing long white teeth with prominent canines.

"Nope, it's me," Miriam said, because he hadn't taken his eyes off her, as if he expected an answer. His eyes were a funny shade of light green blue.

"He asked for it. They can't put a charge on me if he asked for it." The boy's body kept moving even when his legs stopped. His shoulders clenched, his head bobbed, his hands fluttered over his chest, his arm muscles flexed under his smooth, hairless skin. "You saw it, right? I kicked his ass."

"You've got blood on your hand," she told him.

"You're the girl from cooking class," he said. "Student leadership. You think you're going to change the world with your little posters?"

"That was a nice kid you beat up," Miriam said.

"I'll do it again," he said. He took a step toward her. "Tell you what: I'm gonna knock your teeth out and put them in a blender. I'm gonna stuff you in a vending machine. I'll staple you to railroad tracks and let larvae eat you. You'll squirm all around begging. Please, Mylan, shoot me. Please, I don't want to live."

Miriam laughed. She couldn't help it. "You sound like the bad guy in a cartoon. So mean."

The boy cocked his head. "I can be nice, too," he said. His hands were fists. This was what she'd been afraid of all along. Not pain, but that he could claw her face or poke out her eye or disfigure her in some other permanent way that she'd have to carry with her long after she escaped to somewhere better. He or any one of a hundred others, just as volatile.

"Don't touch me," Miriam said. "I'll yell."

Mylan clasped Miriam to his chest. She couldn't move. She struggled and he gripped her tighter. He smelled sweet and rotten.

"Shh," he said, "Be quiet."

A boy had never held her against his chest like this. She felt the warmth through his torn T-shirt. He was so tall her head was level with his armpit. The hair under his arms was silky and fine, like a baby's scalp. She relaxed, because what else could she do? His fingers dug into her shoulders.

He dipped his head low so he could whisper in her ear. His chin bone jabbed her cheek. "I could hurt you bad right now," he said.

Miriam kissed him. She'd never kissed anyone before, except her mother and father. She'd imagined that when she kissed a boy his lips would be hot and hard, but this boy's lips weren't. He released her arms and jerked away from her. Miriam nearly bolted, and could even picture her rush into English class late without a pass, imagine breathing heavy while trying to respond to a question about which door was which in "The Lady, or the Tiger?" But instead she grabbed Mylan's torso and drew him toward her again. She sucked at his bottom lip, bumped her tongue along his teeth. She kept going until he relaxed into her embrace. It was the only thing she could do, until the vice principal found them like that.

Elegy for Organ in Ten Parts

LATELY ELIZABETH DRANK A LOT, so she worried about her liver. Cirrhosis, scarring, nodules, lesions, swelling—all invisible. How could she know what happened inside her body while she ate (little) and slept (less), while she swilled vodka tonics and took home strange men? She didn't usually concern herself with health. Instead, she turned her attention to understated status handbags and baroque skincare regimens. She wondered if the new cruise line campaign at the agency where she worked had the right balance of hip Adams Morgan newness and staid Georgetown sameness, so the Georgetown folks (the target market, obviously) were seduced but not scared. Her masterstroke: buying the rights to "London Calling" for the European Adventure theme song. Now that the project was winding down, she could relax when she got back to the apartment. But no. Her mind revved up and refused to downshift, she would say, if she were trying to sell her brain to eighteen to thirty-five-year-old men, a group she currently loathed after Terence dumped her on New Year's, right before the ball dropped. She'd yelled something to him about how at least she didn't have to wait for his balls to drop, too, now—mean and a little nonsensical, but at least she'd stood up for herself.

As long as her mind had to gnaw something, a bodily organ was good to chew. It mattered more than moisturizer and it showed Elizabeth's burgeoning depth. Or at least her concern for deeper things from a literal, subcutaneous standpoint. Was this what maturity meant? She'd waited twenty-two years to feel the tug of womanly responsibility, ever since her little girl days, shuffling in her mother's pink houndstooth pumps, tripping over long strands of pearls she'd twined around her neck, holding an imaginary cigarette to her mouth and puckering. "Take my calls, Jason," she'd croon to an imaginary secretary in a voice as low as Bea Arthur's, "I'm headed to lunch." Her mother thought this routine was so hilarious that she had Elizabeth repeat it until the joy wore off.

One Thursday evening, Elizabeth prepared a whole chicken for roasting in her postage stamp–sized oven in her business envelope–sized apartment. Her guests—friends from work—would arrive in an hour and a half. The chicken was necessary. She'd promised them a taste of midwestern home cooking. Earlier, she enjoyed some wine to get warmed up, only to find herself drunk with an empty bottle, ready to perform hostess duties as long as her equilibrium held out. She felt as light and free as a paper ribbon whipping on a county-fair parade float.

The chicken's pinkish-white epidermis, only mostly defrosted, matched her own. Elizabeth pondered what lurked beneath her smooth skin, which had the color sucked out due to fifteen years under SPF 60+. As she dug into the bird's frosty insides, she extricated crunchy kidneys, purplish residue, and a mystery chunk. A giblet, perhaps? What was a giblet? Did she have a giblet? Chickens, if her liberal arts education did not deceive her, were close relatives of humans. Not so close as the pig, but still closer than, say, moss or lizards. Therefore, the lumps inside the chicken likely matched those within her. A revelation. The scant times when she considered her bodily composition before, she'd imagined a loaf of French bread, albeit a toned, lithe loaf. A smooth crust with a spongy center. And some blood in there somewhere. Veins. Certainly veins. The thought of organs—such grim masses—nestled beneath her rib cage, occasionally spurting forth bile or lymph, terrified her.

She tossed the chicken into the garbage can and served shrimp instead. When she opened the door to her guests, she said: "I hope you've brought wine." They had. To hew to a prairie theme, she called the shrimp "locusts of the ocean" and insisted her guests do likewise. That night she drank a whole bottle of champagne. She awoke on the couch, a shrimp tail caught in her hair and the knees of her fishnets ripped. She remembered laughing and laughing as the ceiling fell away.

2

Elizabeth set aside the day after this latest drinking binge for virtue. She finished household tasks she'd been putting off. She drank gallons of water and ate pounds of fruits and vegetables, so many that they filled her stomach and piled up in her throat. And she vacuumed. The swoosh of the machine over the rugs, its uneven grumble, the flex of her skinny arm as she pushed, the even stripes furrowed in the carpet: perfection.

She wished she could take a peek at her liver and see how it was doing. Scarred black and brittle like the lungs of a sixty-five-year-old who smoked three packs a day of Marlboro Reds since age twelve, or healthy, gooey purple? She'd never know. A coroner performing a postmortem might know. He'd remove the organ from the T-shaped incision in her belly and drop it on a counterbalance and record its weight in grams on a spreadsheet. The question then, of course, would be cause of death. Had she expired in a car crash, or caught a heel in a crack and pitched into an open manhole? Had her heart failed at the age of eighty-seven, or had she lost her way on a tarmac and stumbled into a jet engine? Maybe the way she had died destroyed her liver, making it impossible to determine its relative health. Evisceration. Defenestration. Conflagration. Only time would tell, and she, very sadly, could never. Or could she?

Elizabeth didn't have a doctor in the city. Or health insurance, for that matter. She called her old doctor in Temperance, Kansas, her hometown. A pediatrician, Dr. Marr had seen Elizabeth through chicken pox, stitches in her ankle, hypoglycemia, and her first birth control prescription. Elizabeth pictured the old woman at home in her favorite chair by a snapping fire, puffing an imaginary pipe. Dr. Marr had given up the real pipe years ago, but the muscle memory, the crooked fingers raised hopefully up to her drooping mouth only to fall back to the edge of her overstuffed armchair, would remain. She spoke deliberately, as always, and she did not sound surprised to hear from Elizabeth. "Short of going in for a biopsy, which would be pricey, there is no way to be absolutely certain. Of course, blood tests could determine how well your cat's liver is processing the material that enters it. But when there are no overt indications of liver sickness, such as jaundice visible at the tips of the ears, there really is no sense in worrying, or worse, undergoing an invasive procedure. So you stop it now, Lizzy. Your kitty's fine. Promise that you'll find her a vet there in D.C., though. We sure are proud of you here. When are you coming home?"

Home was a place of wheat fields like quicksand that stymied her volition. Visiting meant danger, the first step toward meeting a nice man named Timothy, who worked the land, whom she'd have to stand beside with dusty teeth in times of drought and locust clouds, who'd impregnate her over and over and over again, until she'd wear formless shift dresses made of faded flour sacks and shout out that dinner was ready to the front yard, where her babies played on a dirt pile, tossing clods. Dinner would always be beef.

Elizabeth would never come home. Not without a return ticket. Her college roommate, Miriam, a fellow Kansan, had just taken a teaching job at a rural elementary school in western Kansas. Miriam's parents had died, both in the past year, and Elizabeth suspected this new job was a weird form of mourning. Miriam said she should come visit the town, which was named Culvert, anytime she liked. Not Elizabeth. She'd drop in on Kansas once a year, at Christmas, packing oddities to midwestern eyes: yerba mate, pear brandy, smoked fish, and yes, the most expensive-looking clothing she owned. Between black ballerina flats and magenta croco-embossed pumps, of course the pumps would win out. Obviously. They were like Aston Martins for her feet. They said, Hello there, I've been successful in a big city back east. And you?

What was she doing now, inventing a sick pet, calling her child-hood doctor, disturbing the old woman's evening? She was just trying to take care of herself. Same thing as the self-breast exams and mole inspections. She'd heard that high-powered executives with lots money to redistribute got a yearly ultraphysical, which tested for every possible bodily complaint, from colitis to ketosis to cancer. It took two full days to complete. She wasn't that lucky.

As Elizabeth waited for telltale aches in her midsection, she washed her windows using wadded up newsprint and watered-down vinegar. She did the dishes by hand because they got cleaner that way.

3

Friday again, and Elizabeth, drunk, itched for a shower. She'd been at a party in a loft downtown hosted by a band, and they all smoked, and her hair stunk. Someone called Slade who drove a big-ass SUV with custom leather seating had dropped her off back at her place, and she immediately shook up a martini in a highball glass and topped it with five fat green olives. "Baby, one more, just one more. I don't want the night to end," she murmured as she fished the olives one at a time from the jar, her lips heavy and lush on her teeth. Slade had said something similar when he'd tried to invite himself up. He used to be in a band. Used to. She shucked off her dress, turned some knobs, and stepped into the warm mist of the shower, her drink in one hand, loofah in another.

The glass fell and shattered across the bathroom tile. Gin ran down her recently shaved legs. It stung. She cussed and teetered out, sitting on the floor while she picked up the chunks of glass. She nicked her finger—a flesh wound. At least the gin had sterilized the glass. The blood welled up in a merry little pool, and she staunched it with toilet paper. Very sharp glass.

What was to prevent her from making a little slice in her side so she could take a gander at that liver of hers? Just to knock-knock and say hello neighbor. In ancient times . . . When, exactly? The past. She didn't know. The online encyclopedia didn't say. Folks who were long dead now thought the liver was the seat of greed and desire, the part in her, for example, that yearned for a well-cut silk tunic, a shrunken lamb-skin jacket bristling with studs and zippers.

More importantly, though, the liver told your fortune. Bloated with blood, its meanings were opaque. But maybe if she shed some light on the organ, she could read the toxins' etching, the messages on the lobes.

From her recent studies of anatomical maps, done during down-times at work, she knew right where her liver should be. It was truly hard to miss, the largest organ in the human body, aside from the skin. Any cut in the neighborhood of her right thoracic cavity would hit pay-dirt. The protective shroud of peritoneum would need to be shrugged aside, but now her body felt numb, preanesthetized.

Well? She raised the shard to her belly and pressed the point into her flesh. Lifted away, it left a small red indentation, a pressure mark rather than a perforation. She would have to push much harder.

She passed out with her left leg twisted under her. It took ten minutes to get the blood flowing back to her foot in the morning.

4

At a New Year's party at a club called Privilege, which was done up like an English manor house and filled with staff dressed like Jeeves or naughty French maids, while picking up her Brandy Alexander at the bar, Elizabeth had met this man, Chef Dave. He owned a fusion bistro in Shaw and said he was poised to be the next chef-lebrity. The chef rocked back and forth and tapped his foot, as though to his own personal hip-hop soundtrack. Elizabeth stood stock-still to make a point. Encircling his wrist was a magnetic bracelet that, she supposed, he wore for its healing powers. A man-jewel of the silver and turquoise variety swallowed his right index finger. Higher up on his arm, he had a tattoo: a worried ham hopping down the street, pursued by a carving knife and fork. He had a bit of a belly, and Elizabeth imagined the flames from the gas stoves at his restaurant tickling his gut as he stretched to stir a roux on a back burner. She wondered what his flesh might smell like as it burned. When he found out she was a fellow midwesterner, he invited her to dinner at his place, and Elizabeth accepted. He reminded her of a boy she dated in high school, who had sweaty palms and a six-pack, who stared at her naked body and told her, guile-free, that it was the most beautiful thing he'd ever seen. Chef Dave's goodness, his realness, was hard to spot in the city. And she did value a home-cooked meal.

5

Lately, Elizabeth wore men's cologne. Maybe she was lonely. She'd spent an afternoon at the fragrance counter frustrating a sharply dressed saleswoman with her indecision. Her brother, the ostensible recipient of this ostensible gift of scent, was picky about his personal fragrances. He needed something really masculine, with no sweet or citrusy notes. She decided on a blocky bottle of Gucci, which contained notes of pepper, ginger, amber, and woods, and the relieved clerk rang up her sale in record time, lest Elizabeth change her mind again. The scent surprised Elizabeth. She thought amber was a gemstone from which one could also extract recombinant DNA in order to fashion huge animatronic dinosaurs, which went wild and ate people. Also: "woods"? What sort of woods? Conifer? Parquet flooring? Golf club? Number two pencil?

She relished being wrapped in a veil of simulated woods, though. Her very own wilderness retreat. She would breathe in, and as she exhaled, the air caught in her throat like suede over a hacksaw. She was so rough and delicious, so butch and ladylike.

The problem here in D.C. was that she was so far from anything real. Sometimes, especially when the sun reflected sharply off the pavement and the city sky was awash in pure, white light, Elizabeth yearned for Kansas, coarse and homelike. The same impulse lured investment bankers to shovel horseshit on dude ranches. A uniquely American experience existed elsewhere and she was missing it. She had grown up in a small town in the middle of the country and moved to a large city on the East Coast, her nation's capital, and she could only guess at the geography that lay between the two. She'd never cared before.

Elizabeth pictured her life in this nowhere place, this county seat of authenticity and true American treasure. She would drive an old car, a convertible, with a big, skinny steering wheel with finger grips. At twilight, the sinking sun tinged everything—the scrubby trees she whizzed past, the road, her hands on the wheel—vivid yellow. Like jaundice. She wore a clean flannel shirt, a bit frayed at the elbows. Maybe Miriam rode shotgun. Their destination: a roadside honky-tonk, tin-sided and encrusted with twinkling Christmas lights, where Elizabeth was a regular, where muscly men and women arm wrestled for drinks, and where she was welcomed by nickname. In this life, Elizabeth was always young, always single—not shiftless, but free, and always one drink away from stumbling onto the point of things, sharp as a dart tip, familiar as the scent of unwashed bedding. She felt this place deep down. She felt it in her liver.

6

Elizabeth blacked out in her leather armchair, still wearing the black dress and purple tights she wore to work. Her head hung forward, bobbing up and down with each breath, her earrings brushing her bare shoulders. She jerked her head up periodically then slid back into smooth, drunken slumber. But the twitches wouldn't pass, so she teetered to her feet to get some orange juice. The thick liquid washed away the taste of moldering gin and left instead a tang that raised her eyebrows. She smoothed her forehead with her thumb. She tried to avoid unnecessary facial expressions because she'd read that it took only a thousand creasings of the skin, a thousand smiles or inquisitive eyebrow twitches, before the lines of age marked her.

She knew she wouldn't be able to sleep unless she determined the source of her uneasiness. The trick was to scoop the worry up and slop it on a page, her pen a trowel, her insides a barrow of wet cement. The angst had to be spread before it dried and hardened. She found a pen and notebook in her purse, crawled back under the table, and sprawled between midcentury wooden legs, wrote.

7

When Elizabeth tried to raise her face from her wood floor the next morning, it stuck. Her cheek had landed in a puddle of orange juice, and she had to peel her face free like the price tag from the sole of a new shoe. The scene that greeted her was not one of simple abundance, which was a shame, because that was what she hoped her dining area would evoke. The orange juice carton lay overturned on a side table, dripping sticky sweetness onto her fluffy Moroccan rug. She had a bad bruise on her calf.

She picked up her notebook and read:

- New Campaign: Giovanni's table wine
- Sweeter than others = more calories
- Spin this: bottle in print ad looks like big lollipop or peppermint candy? Bottle carried by girl in candy striper outfit? Giovanni's in the IV bags? Alcohol as medicine? Is this offensive?
- Tagline: How Sweet!
- Commercial, use tagline to mean a thoughtful gift: hot Good Samaritan (shirtless?) helps old lady cross street. When they get to other side, he hands her a mini bottle, like airline size. Close-up on her wrinkled face. She says: "How sweet!" Bottle or Samaritan? Both. Works both ways!

8

Chef Dave sliced foie gras for the two of them. Fancy little crackers stood at the ready, and a bottle of white wine perspired on his granite countertop. Elizabeth wanted that wine. Chef Dave told her a funny story about custard as he whisked the knife over the lobed gray hunks, which fell in perfect tablets before her. As he set the knife down, she changed her mind. She wanted the knife.

Chef Dave glided toward her like a waiter, the wine bottle clutched proudly in his hands. For a moment, he looked dashing, but then he tripped. He grabbed for the counter and spilled the wine. Thick drops ran down the granite as he steadied himself.

"Good thing you didn't spill it all. That wine's the only reason I'm sticking around," she said. Chef Dave laughed even though her joke was mean. As he wiped the counter, she slid the foie gras knife from the cutting board to her lap. She clicked her pinky nail against the blade in a rat-tat-tat, rat-tat-tat rhythm. The top of her hand pressed the granite. Which was cooler, smoother? The blade or the stone? She knew which was sharper.

9

"I've got to show you my artifacts!" Chef Dave announced as he approached from behind. Elizabeth wore nothing. Chef Dave wore only a pair of boxer shorts with lobsters on them. "Better than crabs," he'd joked earlier, as they'd stripped.

He pulled her up from the bed and led her across the stone floors, past the kitchen and the low-slung living room furniture, to a door she had not noticed before.

"I don't show people this room very often," Chef Dave said. "Most would never understand something like this."

She expected a sex dungeon, but instead, he threw open the door to an ideal midwestern den. The walls were covered in wood paneling, and the floor with shaggy green carpeting. Dead, preserved animals eyed her. Flat surfaces were encrusted with arrowheads and puzzling ancient iron tools like barnacles on sea rocks. The fireplace screen was crafted of barbed wire, and more strands hung framed on the walls. Each was neatly labeled with the pattern and year: Curtis Twins 1892, Ellwood Spread 1882, Frentless 1875, Watkins Lazy Plait 1876, Merrill Twirl 1871.

"Ellwood Spread. Those sound like cowboy names," Elizabeth said. "What is this place?"

"My dad had a room just like this. He'd go in after dinner and shut the door. I don't know what he did after that. I usually just read. Pour a little finger of scotch. I got a lot of this stuff from him when he died. He hunted, fished—really loved the land. We're from Nebraska."

Eye to eye with a duck decoy on a shelf, Elizabeth told Chef Dave, "It's lovely." She meant it. The room awakened something deep in her gut, some rumbling she couldn't hush.

10

Back in the cold, gray bedroom, Chef Dave had already fallen asleep. His mouth fell open and a demisnore rose from his lips. He lay balled up, his hand cradling his dick through his boxers.

Elizabeth delicately set her feet down and followed the path back to the den. She got off track and rammed her shin into a coffee table's sharp corner before she found her bearings.

She put her hand to the doorknob and pushed. Smells of old hides and new leather rushed out from the den. She reached for the light switch, but her hand grazed bare wall. Panic collapsed her chest, in this strange room in the dark, so unlike the rest of the apartment. She groped toward the tables of artifacts, panting and searching for a lamp. Her fingers closed around a remote control. She mashed some buttons, and the fireplace whooshed alive.

She gasped. Before, there had been too much to take in, and all that registered was metal, stone, and fur. But now, the fire threw bob-

bing shadows on the walls and made the room cavelike, cozily primitive. A bear stood fully erect in a corner, his black glass eyes glinting
in the firelight. Trophies with leaping fish on golden lines rose from
the coffee table. The air smelled of tanned leather and lemon Pledge.
A glassed-in gun rack was filled to capacity, and ammo belts flanked
it. She took the foie gras knife from her purse and laid it beside the
objects on a velvet display table: the hatchet, the bow and arrow, the
hammer, the flint knife points. Hackers, scrapers, piercers, saws,
they were not made for delicate work like her knife—a trim modern
marvel.

She thought in a loopy, warm way now. Wine saturated her brain.
That knife, this room, were part of her, as was her new male friend,
whose face she'd caressed and patted as if it were her own. She could
imagine this room thousands of years ago; its walls stone, she just
one in a chain of its dwellers. Drumbeats mingled with the crackling
fire, and men and women circled that fire, coaxing flames to blister
the flesh of their kills. The meat would sear their tongues. They would
wipe their hands on their loins, then go out and hunt some more. If
they had bad livers, they would not have been chickenshits. They'd
have investigated for themselves. Her liver throbbed. Elizabeth in-
haled deeply, grabbed up the stolen knife, and held the blade in the
fire to sanitize it. With her other hand, she stroked her midsection,
figuring out where she needed to cut. "Some light on the subject,"
she whispered. She lifted the knife an inch away from the flames and
stared at the blade. It shined like it had absorbed all the glow of the
fire.

Her hand was like an extension of the knife. The knife guided her
hand to her side. Her other hand stroked the skin over the organ. It
didn't feel like her hand. It felt like many hairy-knuckled hands that
smelled of trail dust and animal blood.

The palm passed over the flesh, and the knife followed behind, eas-
ing through the membrane, severing capillaries, and digging into
the thin layer of adipose tissue, the heat cauterizing as it cut. Blood
dripped down to the line of her lacy panties, where the flow joined a

seam's path to her hip. The hot fluid slid from the point of her hipbone to the carpet, where it burrowed into the fibers. Her fingers closed over her side, and blood rose through the cracks between them. She moved her hand to take a look.

A New Man

JIM DIDN'T SMELL DIFFERENT. He didn't taste different when Patty kissed him. He talked in the usual gruff way, as if speaking pained him. He still had trouble making eye contact. He still watched TV in the blue leather recliner. His small eyes never left the screen while she tidied around him, and when she asked if he wanted to talk to their son, Clay, when he called, he still shook his head no.

Now he snacked from a bag of whole walnuts. He shattered each one against the coffee table with a ball-peen hammer from the hardware store and picked delicately through the debris for the meats. That was different.

When Patty walked over by him to water the African violet on top of the TV, she heard it. Humming. His breath was quieter lately because his lungs were more efficient, so she noticed right away. "What are you humming, hon?" she asked.

"Humming? Who hums?"

"You do, I guess. Just now."

He grunted.

~~~~~

</div>

Two weeks ago, a doctor had outlined the new rules as Jim lay groggy in his hospital bed, a dressing wrapping the wound on his chest, tubes funneling antirejection serum into his forearm. A good diet. A strict regimen of pills. No straining. No working at the store. No leaving the house for the first few months to minimize infection risk. Patty wrote it all down. Jim's body could reject the lung anytime, and when it did, it wouldn't be on her conscience.

※※※

When Patty was sixteen, she and her friends Crystal and Della used to lean against the stage in the drama classroom before school, critiquing hallway fashions and ranking potential boyfriends. One day Jim walked in and asked Patty to go to the homecoming dance with him. For all the girls' bold talk, their worldly knowledge ended with ruching and madras plaid. Della laughed nervously. Jim looked right in Patty's eyes, his lips quivering. Her first impulse was no, but there was no way to say it politely. Jim was quiet and tall. Well liked. His family owned a hardware store in town. Her family was poor. There was nothing wrong with him. She said okay.

Cool, Jim had said and exited stage right. That was him. Self-assured to the point of showing no emotion. The only reason she had for saying no was that saying yes would make her life different, and she liked her life. But she'd said yes, and her friends replayed the scene until class began. Had he winked when he said cool? He had. No, he hadn't. Yes, he had and it was hot. Crystal and Della made Jim a romantic hero, his taciturnity a product of unfathomed depths instead of a blank mind. They told her how lucky she was. Later she'd wished his eye would have fallen on another girl.

※※※

Now, a couple decades later, Jim's friends all looked up to him. When Jim's doctor still allowed Jim to go to the hardware store, Jim's friends would gather there, spinning stories about ladies they'd met in bars, and Jim would sit back and wait for his moment. For example, one time Patty overheard a guy talking about how he was sad because his goldfish had died. The other guys were comforting him or trying to ignore him, and Jim said, "Sounds like dinner. Hold on, I think I've got a really small grill in back somewhere." Everybody died laughing. Jim said one thing per every ten things each of his friends said, but when he did speak, it was really mean. Since the surgery, though, he'd been even quieter. Besides saying hello, who are you, and where am I when he woke up in intensive care, his lips were sealed. Sometimes his chest ballooned up and his eyes darted left and right as if he were dying to speak, but when Patty leaned close, nothing but air hissed out.

<center>~~~~~</center>

Patty wondered just how much Jim did feel. What must it be like to have someone else's lung in you? The doctor said Jim would notice a bit of tightness in the new lung, that more effort would be needed to inflate it at first. Soon his body would adjust. But lungs were unlike any other organs. A kidney or liver did its work whether you thought of it or not. You could monitor your breathing, though; you'd know you drew air into a dead man's lung inside you. Patty hoped Jim never thought that way. It was enough to make someone never want to take another breath.

That night, after she'd tidied up the dinner dishes and Jim had finished watching his programs, Patty listened to him snoring beside her in bed.

The humming. Now she heard it again, low and velvety. She thought she caught a word, a couple words: "city . . . lover." Jim never listened to music. He'd been dividing his time between sleep and TV since he'd arrived home.

Patty whispered, "Keep singing, sweetheart." When they first got married, they'd lie in bed at night and Patty would talk about what she'd done that day, and what she wanted to do tomorrow, and the next week, and the next year. Jim was so patient. He'd say yep occasionally to let her know he was listening.

Patty squeezed his arm, and he really opened up, drawling from deep in his belly, "Smooth Operator." He coughed and flipped to his side, facing away from Patty. How the hell did Jim know that song? He wasn't exactly into music.

Patty had heard that song at the beauty shop. She didn't know many lyrics, so Jim couldn't have picked them up from her. The radio in his truck was broken, and he watched only reruns of *M*A*S*H* or *The Andy Griffith Show* on television. They had no CD or tape player, which now that she thought about it, seemed silly, because she for one did like music. Maybe it was from a commercial. But that didn't make sense because he knew too much of the song, way more than the thirty seconds or so a commercial featured.

There was no way those lyrics came from his new lung, were stored there by the muscle memory of the organ's previous owner, who was a fan of Sade. That was impossible.

Was Sade all the lung knew? Or was the organ like a fleshy jukebox? She prodded Jim a couple of times to see if he'd sing more, but he groaned and she felt guilty. She could try again tomorrow night. She hadn't looked forward to a night in bed with Jim in twenty-four and a half years.

wwww

Their son, Clay, used to call Patty often when he knew Jim was at work. They'd talk about how their day was going, and a few months ago, Clay had started telling her that she'd be better off without Jim. Patty had honestly never entertained that option. They'd been together for so long. She and Clay had one conversation where she'd said that if Jim was keeping him from coming home, Clay should just tell her, and she'd leave Jim.

Clay didn't say anything, and then Jim had gotten sick. The next time they'd talked, she explained how things were, how she couldn't possibly leave Jim while he was ailing. Get a nurse, Clay said. I can't,

Patty said. Clay didn't call for several weeks after that, and her calls to him went to voicemail. She was a little relieved that Jim's illness had settled the thing. There was no decision left for her to make. Maybe that new lung would get Jim thinking about dying, about how if everyone's going to croak ultimately, he might as well treat his only son nice.

uww

In the morning, her enthusiasm lagged. One good night with Jim among thousands, while he was unconscious no less, didn't mean a lot. Maybe she could make a life without Jim. She could rent a little cottage close to downtown, find a job as a secretary at an insurance office or at a law firm again. Get a kitty cat. Jim was allergic. She'd spend her free time decorating, painting the bathroom pink and the living room mint green. It'd be so quiet in there. The television would gather dust. She thought about this as she cooked Jim's breakfast—eggs, bacon, and sausage. He wasn't listening to doctors' orders regarding diet, and she was abetting him.

She took Jim a plate, still halfway thinking about the cottage, but then she saw him. His eyes were squeezed shut under gray lids. Jim needed her right now. She'd guide him through this then think about herself. If only he hadn't started humming. That humming gave her hope, a cruel hope that kept her knotted to him. And then someday there would be no time left, and all she'd have been was wife to Jim.

uww

Jim and Patty started dating after homecoming. Every Friday night, he'd honk for her in his pickup truck a couple of hours before game time and they'd drive to the stadium. She'd sit in the stands and watch the boys warm up, knitting a striped scarf in their school colors. Then, after the game, she waited with the other girlfriends for the team to emerge from the locker room. She liked the girls but couldn't help but think she was above them. Jim had chosen her, and he had his pick of anyone. It was no real choice at all, he'd told her. Tracy was a slut, and Deena had a pinhead, and Sarah was stupid, and Julie's teeth were crooked, and Ann's tits were too small. Luckily, Patty was perfect in his eyes. Not too dumb, and plenty pretty. She tried to think about the boys the same way, but she failed every time. Adam's eyes drifted toward his nose, but they were the sweetest blue. You hardly noticed one of Jack's legs was shorter than the other when he ran at full speed. Nothing wrong with any of those boys.

She'd fall to imagining the boys together in the shower, soaping each other's backs and touching each other's firm pectoral muscles softly, getting caught up in the feel of the skin stretched tight over hard abs, then punching to make up for it. She could almost see the bright backsides where towel snapped flesh, the way the long snapper might give the QB a hand job after a poor game while the other players watched and smiled. The coach might say, "Circle up, boys. We've got some jerking to do." The players would spring to action, as though that's what they'd been waiting for all game. Longer, in fact. All week, since they'd last had their hands on each other. That's what Patty thought about after the game.

Then Jim would emerge, smelling of good, honest soap and just the vaguest hint of sweat and turf. They'd drive out to Coronado Heights and draw beers from the keg someone's parents bought. There was a lookout spot with a little castle the WPA had built in the thirties and a bluff where you could see the rock layers that proved Kansas used to be an ocean. The sandstone was soft enough you could carve your initials in it. The hill was called Coronado Heights because that's where Coronado gave up his search for the seven cities of gold and decided to head back down to Mexico. Patty wondered what it was about this spot that had made him sure there was no treasure here. It was pretty.

One night, Jim and Patty snuck off beneath the bluff. Patty slid her arm up Jim's shirt, rubbing the smooth skin on his chest. She leaned in and whispered, "I think about you while I'm waiting after the game."

"Yeah?" Jim said.

"You with all of those other men, all naked in the showers. I like to imagine what you do in there." Jim shoved her away. She hit her head on the bluff and must have lost consciousness for a few seconds. The roar of an engine woke her. She lay on her face snorting dust. Her nose was skinned. Her scalp had a damp spot. When she scrambled up the hillside, Jim's pickup was gone. She parted her hair on the other side so the blood wouldn't show and joined her friends around the keg. They asked what happened. She said she must have fallen. They said no, what happened to Jim. She said she didn't know.

A month later, she thought she might be pregnant, and two months later, she was sure of it. Five weeks after that, Patty and Jim got married. She was sixteen. He'd done that one bad thing, pushing her, but so frequently men did worse. And they inherited that hardware store, so they didn't want for money.

*

The night after Jim sang for the first time, Patty waited for him to sleep. She anticipated Sade again, but instead, he sang Madonna's "Like a Prayer." She and Clay used to sing along to that song in the car on the way to his T-ball practices. Toward the chorus, Jim's voice turned hoarse and he tripped over some words. Patty snuggled up to him and put the weight of her legs on Jim's so he couldn't flip over. She whispered the lyrics in his ear. It was thrilling how their voices wove. After verse two, Patty let him rest. His body was hot. She turned on the bedside lamp to see him better. His face was bright red. She lifted his shirt and warmed her palms on his skin.

*

Her family hadn't been that poor. If only she hadn't gotten pregnant. She could have earned a scholarship. A good job. She wouldn't have stuck around contending with Jim for so long if they hadn't had Clay, that was for sure. Was Jim bad, though? That was the part that always confused her. She knew he wasn't ideal. They couldn't talk to each other, but no one can, really. Not in any sort of perfect way. There would always be misunderstandings, like at Coronado Heights.

Clay couldn't stand Jim. Clay had moved out to the East Coast a week after he finished high school for a liberal arts college, where he studied business and women's and gender studies. He'd stayed back east every summer. He had a string of boyfriends Patty learned about through his posts on social media. She'd tried to talk to Clay about those handsome young men she supposed he loved, but he was very private, which she could understand with Jim, but not with her.

Clay's long hours at work prevented him from keeping in touch as much as he'd like. Patty hadn't seen him since his best friend's wedding last year, an occasion he couldn't miss. When she'd called to tell him about the transplant, he'd asked primly, "Is it absolutely essential that I'm there?" Patty admitted it was not. A few days after the surgery, Clay had posted online some pictures of himself and other fit young men on a boat. They were labeled "Kanopolis Lake Lifeguards Reunion!" Kanopolis was twenty miles away from where Jim lay ailing. She got the sense that maybe they both were waiting for Jim to die. Maybe then their relationship could improve. Maybe everything would improve.

༄༅

Patty started to tease Jim, singing snatches of songs he'd covered the previous evening as she dusted or did dishes. At first it disappointed her that he never reacted, but then she came to appreciate their secret life, she and sleeping Jim with that magical lung. Even awake, Jim got better. Most of the time when he sat in front of the TV, he didn't even watch. His eyelids drooped, his pupils dilated, his hands hung at his sides. All that moved were his chest and the lungs inside it, which never stopped their rise and fall.

༄༅

She considered calling the doctor to report Jim's singing, but she didn't. There was nothing unhealthy about song, and she was afraid the doctor would make the singing go away. Jim performed better at night when he had the antirejection dose early in the morning. One day she didn't give it to him at all, and in return she got "Burnin' for You." Now she tried to stagger the days without a dose, so there weren't too many in a row. Anyway, Jim was certainly capable of remembering for himself to take his medicine.

wmmw

One day Patty ran some errands and returned to find Jim scrunched in his chair cradling the cordless phone to his ear with both hands. He made warbly sounds into the receiver. She took the phone, raised it to her own ear, and said hello.

"What happened to Dad?" Clay asked.

Patty bent over Jim and said, "Jesus, Jim, what have you been saying?"

"No, he's like a zombie," Clay told her. "He said, like, 'Hello,' and just stopped talking. I heard this humming noise. Was that him?"

Patty took a closer look at her glassy-eyed husband. She waved a hand across his field of vision. He blinked twice but didn't follow the movement. "Well, yes, actually. He's different since the operation. He hums now. Doesn't talk but hums."

"Maybe you should talk to the doctor."

"Well, I hadn't thought about doing that, really. It's pretty pleasant. He hasn't said anything mean in weeks."

"As long as you're happy," Clay said.

"You know what? I am."

That night, the two of them tore up "I Will Survive." Afterward Jim cried.

"What's wrong, darling?" Patty asked, rubbing his back.

"So sad. So, so sad," he mumbled. "I don't know where I am."

Patty held him tight. "It's okay. You just cry. I'll always be here beside you." He struggled for a second, but then he snuggled his head into her breasts, and his body relaxed. She rocked him back and forth, blowing softly in his hair, which when she nestled her nose in it, smelled of good honest soap and turf.

Jim was different now, Patty was sure of it. All the bad times were over. They slept that way, with Jim's head tucked against her chest, their legs entwined, all night long.

wmmm

When Patty woke, Jim was staring at her. He sat up in bed and pulled her arm. She got up. He led her into the garage and pointed at the car. She heard him go back inside and drawers opening and shutting in the kitchen. She sat down in the passenger's seat. Jim always insisted on driving. He came out holding a balled-up sweatshirt.

"It's not cold, Jim," she said.

He opened the driver-side door and walked around to the passenger side, where he opened that door, too.

"You want me to drive?"

He nodded. Patty got in the driver's seat and pulled the car out. "Where are we going?" she asked. He pointed the way with an arm stiff like a dowsing rod. Whenever he wanted her to turn, he'd grunt and swing the arm to the left or right. At first Patty tried to guess what he was after. "You want a milkshake at Bogey's, Jim? Maybe we're going by the hardware store so we can see how the guys are doing without you?" He ignored her.

Soon they were running out of town. Halfway to Lindsborg, he pointed to a little road leading up a hill.

Coronado Heights. They hadn't been there since that night he'd pushed her down. The place hadn't changed. The castle looked just the same, a little pathetic all by itself on the hill. The day was one of the first warm ones of the year, and Patty rolled down her window as they drove up to the parking area. Theirs was the only car. The wind whipped Patty's hair into her face as she helped Jim out of the car. She told him again it was too warm for a sweatshirt, but he wouldn't put down his little bundle.

"Let's go see if we can find our names on the bluff," Patty said, but Jim pulled her away, into the castle. There was one big room of twenty by twenty feet with some concrete picnic tables. The only light came through slit windows high up the walls. Jim's face looked odd in the shadows. His eyes had widened and his cheeks were thinner. The nose wasn't right. This nose was a straight line, while Jim's ended in a bulb. The lips were thinner than Jim's. Patty couldn't feel her feet and hands. She dropped the keys and Jim picked them up. Sensation rushed back. She held out her hand for the keys, but Jim ignored her. What's this, she thought. Outside the castle, the wind whistled.

In one corner of the room were steps leading up to the tower. Jim climbed and gestured for her to follow. She did. The wind nearly knocked her back down the stairs. When she regained her balance, she saw Jim was leaned against a turret breathing heavily. His pajamas, which she'd bought special for his hospital stay, snapped in the wind.

"Jim?" she said. He turned. His face was just like it had always been. She rushed toward him, but he motioned her back. "Did you overdo it?" she asked. "Those stairs were tough on me, too."

He breathed more and more rapidly. Patty tried to pat his back or rub it—anything to calm him. But he pushed her away and kept on, panting almost impossibly fast. She counted three breaths a second. Surely he would pass out. He hadn't had his medicine that morning or the night before.

His eyes rolled up behind the lids. Patty positioned herself to catch him when he fell. But he didn't. His torso swelled. At first Patty thought he had just shifted his weight so it looked bigger, but then the pajama top stretched across his inflating chest until the fabric could no longer take the strain. The buttons popped off. Under the cloth the flesh was red. Patty touched it but had to tear her hand away before it scorched her palm. The torso vibrated. The eyes rolled down, but now they were all pupil.

Jim's body bounced up and down. His feet left the ground, and returned, and left again. He floated two feet high. The torso's girth dwarfed his arms, legs, and head. He spun so his feet were pointed up and his head down, which seemed to be the most comfortable position for such a body. He floated higher so his head was level with Patty's, his arms dangling down. "Goodbye," he said. "No more I love you. Goodbye, woman." He rose higher.

Patty caught his wrists to try to draw him back to her, but the sweatshirt he'd been carrying fell away to reveal a ball-peen hammer. He swung it. She retreated. A current caught him and he lifted into the sky. He waved the hammer at her. He drifted across the prairie humming a sweet melody she didn't recognize. He got so small she could barely see him, except for little gleams from the hammer, which he still seemed to flourish.

And didn't she feel light, too? Didn't she draw air into her perfect lungs and hold it until she felt like she might float right away, and push it out like spring cleaning, like giving birth, like a visitor who overstayed his welcome? "Your daddy is gone, Clay," she'd tell her son the next time he called. "He's left me."

Various
Shortcomings
of Mine

WE STAGGERED UP THROUGH THE BRUSH, Ann first, brandy bottle and trowel in hand, and me behind her, clutching the box that held our dead cat, Orvil. We loved him more, perhaps, than humans should love an animal. He had left us before his time, caught under our neighbor's pickup truck. We'd spent the day crying, but now neither of us could stop laughing. The sunlight strained through the trees, dappling Ann's bare shoulders.

"You still got the brandy, Annie?" I called to her.

"Right here, Hank," she said, hoisting the half-gone bottle above her head to tap it with her trowel.

"We're going to bury him on top of a goddamn mountain."

"Hell, yes."

"It will be a sweet funeral, better even than your aunt's."

"If by better you mean drunker," Ann said.

We busted up laughing. We'd been drinking for several hours from a dusty bottle of no-name brandy from our reception two years ago, fished from a back cabinet. There was a reason no one had drunk it. After I took a couple swigs, my lungs wanted to climb out of my throat.

The wooded slope felt warm, the humidity linking our bodies somehow. Deer had used this path, maybe, and poison ivy ringed it. If this were a happier time, I might grab Ann by the torso, edge her toward the trifoliate leaves, say, uh oh, watch out! She'd whack my hands away before we'd kiss.

Right then I was the smartest person in the world, and Annie was second, and when we got home, we'd fuck, maybe on the floor in the kitchen. She'd blindfold me with a dishtowel that smelled like Windex, I'd slap her ass with a spatula, and everything would be all right. We would remember this sad day fondly. We could still have fun. Years from now, Ann would say, Remember when we climbed? I would say, Yes, of course. We sure were something back then. Something? More like something else. You got that right. My aged eyes would crinkle wistfully. She'd say how well I'd acquitted myself that day, tell me that's when she learned just how strong I was.

Now I doubled over, hiccupping with laughter, slipping on accreted layers of rotting leaves. Something else indeed. I had to hold Orvil's casket with both hands, so I couldn't reach to steady myself, and the casket slipped out of my grasp and thumped to the ground.

I scrabbled for Orvil as his box slid down the hill. I caught up to him deep in a poison ivy patch, and I grasped him with all my might. My fingers were studded with splinters.

"You dropped him," Ann said, the joy gone from her voice.

Shit, shit, shit, I thought. That tore it. Sometimes Ann's emotions got to rolling so I couldn't keep up. This would be one of those times. But why? Why did it have to be? Orvil couldn't feel anything. I said I was sorry, for all the good it would do, modulating my tone, articulating like a champ.

"You don't even care, I can tell," Ann said, her voice cracking. She turned and charged up the slope, grabbing low branches for balance. I chose to think she was grieving quietly up ahead, not plotting just the right words for a message very mean and very true to be delivered once I caught up. She turned around and I braced myself.

"You don't even care," she said again. I didn't reply.

She was right, dropping Orvil didn't bother me, but that didn't mean I didn't care he was dead. His passing was so preventable. That was the hard part. I was sure she would point that fact out to me, day after day after day. Even though he was my cat. Or I had found him, at least, outside my office, where I worked as an IT guy at Social Security.

I was smoking outside during a break at work one day when I heard his weak mew. I thought he was a bird, but then I realized the sound came from under a dumpster, so I knelt, slicking my good pants with garbage juice. I lured him with some pickled meat from the office fridge. He emerged, and I couldn't even tell he was orange, he was so dirty, and his body shook. He held his ears back until he got a taste of the meat, which perked him right up. I tucked him in my jacket and zipped him against my chest.

When I got home and unwrapped him, Ann clasped her hands and squealed. Together, Ann and I fed him and cleaned him. We took turns kissing his pink nose. Orvil bit my feet under the covers every morning, piercing the quilt with his teeth. As he grew, he nibbled more gently, so it just tickled. He tried to chew Ann's feet, but she kicked him in her sleep, so he always came back for mine.

Orvil arrived at just the right time for us because Ann had been working up a head of steam about the difference in our salaries. Fair enough, too, because those kids put her through hell. But it wasn't my fault, either, that my steady government job paid better than public school teaching.

"Doesn't it seem ridiculous," Ann had said, "that you fix computers and I mold young lives and society has deemed your work more valuable?"

"Seems from what you tell me," I said, "you do less molding of young lives and more keeping them from beating each other's heads in with xylophone mallets." She wouldn't say anything after that. She had a singing voice so clear and beautiful it about hurt your ears. And she was always knitting some fancy little thing, taking a snarl of yarn and turning it into a doily or a scarf. Something useful. Her many talents were wasted on those elementary music kids—she knew it and I knew it.

We used to talk to each other about any old thing, all the time. This was a few years ago, when we'd first gotten together. She'd tell me her theories about how there was only a finite amount of happiness in the world and it didn't always go to those who deserved it, and I'd teach her the names and calls of all the birds in our yard—cardinal, nuthatch, yellow-bellied flicker. She'd mimic them back at me, and Orvil would perk up, looking for his prey.

Now silence ruled the day. We'd speak until one of us (usually Ann) would get offended. Her go-to line these days was as follows: Nothing's ever perfect. Have you noticed that? Sometimes I'd like to say to her, Yes Ann, I have noticed, and this failure to achieve even a moment of perfection in our brief shared lifetime is surely the fault of both sides, don't you reckon?

I think even Orvil could sense our discord. When Orvil felt nervous, he'd do what we called loafing, because he looked like a loaf of bread, haunches pushed up, paws hooked under the torso. Perfectly self-contained and remote. Ann and I loafed too. We would prod the other one with a paw—either tenderly or hard—then curl back up inside ourselves. Orvil changed us for a while, but then we started to use him against each other, saying things like, Orvil doesn't like it when you listen to that music so loud or You're petting Orvil wrong or Orvil can tell you're lying when you say you love me. One day after Ann had been jabbing at me for an hour about various shortcomings of mine, she said, her hand against a red welt on her cheek, "I can't believe you hit me in front of Orvil."

·∾∾∾·

Orvil wasn't allowed outdoors, but this had been a fine spring, and he'd been so certain that we finally just let him go. He stalked birds, though his bulk and his fur, orange as a warning cone, held him back. He warmed his belly in the sun. He caught spiders. He ate grass, which he puked on the carpet. He had a delicate digestive system.

This very morning, a Sunday, I'd heard him meowing at the back door to get inside—half-heard, really, because I was watching the Royals get shut out on TV. Ann had heard him, too, she told me later, and she thought I had let him in. But she knew how I zoned out. One of her critiques was that I ignored her when the TV was on. Even at restaurants, I'd see a screen glowing over her shoulder and be helpless. Wasn't marriage about accepting each other's failings?

And then our neighbor Jim knocked on our door, head hanging, talking fast. I'd never seen him anything but cocky and brooding like a mean old rooster, so I knew right away something wasn't right. Now he'd shrunk to about half his former size and somehow turned cordial. Ann told me he'd had health problems. Smoking, she'd said, pointing at the pack tucked in my shirt pocket.

Jim cradled a ruffled lump in his arms. His truck idled in our driveway. "I didn't see him," he said hoarsely. "He ran right in front of the truck. I'm so sorry. So very sorry. Please forgive me. He was going after a bird across the street, I think."

I stood gaping for a second before my manners kicked in. I said it was okay, there was nothing he could have done, we never should have let Orvil out in the first place, et cetera, while Ann glared over my shoulder.

I was sorry for Jim. I was sorry for Ann. I was sorry for me. I was very sorry for Orvil. I hoped he hadn't felt any pain.

I had taken Orvil's body, still warm, from Jim's hands, him saying, if there's anything else I could do, and Ann interrupting, saying, you've done enough. I gave Jim a grimace, like, you and me both, friend, and I let the screen swing shut.

Ann ran into the bedroom and closed the door. "You asshole," I heard her yell from inside. Probably wasn't that. Probably was something milder. You. You're a hassle. You rascal. Maybe a burst of patriotism: USA! Nope. Not that.

It didn't seem decent to set Orvil's body in the hallway, so I carried him out to the garage and laid him on my workbench. I found some rough pine boards from the privacy fence Jim and I built together. I held a board beside Orvil to gauge size. His eyes were shut tight. One fang poked from his pink lips. I don't think I could have gone on if his eyes were open.

I fired up my jigsaw. An hour and a half later, I had a lopsided cuboid with a lid that nearly fit, perfect for a cat or, I realized, a baby.

Some blood had spackled my white T-shirt, so I took off my shirt, wadded it, and arranged the fabric like a pillow. I set Orvil inside, tucking his tail around him. He didn't look peaceful. He looked sad. I nailed the coffin shut. I had a beer, then another.

I knocked at the bedroom door. Ann didn't answer right away so I went in and found her folded tight on the bed, clutching her feet in her hands like a monkey. Her face was splotched red. Tears glued strands of hair to her cheeks. I picked her up by the armpits and set her upright. She rolled back down. I scooted her to the edge of the bed and nudged her. She balanced for a second then tipped forward. She took her hands from her feet just in time to catch herself. When she rose back up, she said, "He was just a little animal and now he's dead."

I told her to raid the liquor cabinet because we were going for a drive.

As we sat in our driveway in the Scout, my old off-roader, with boxed-up Orvil in the back seat, Ann asked, "Where are we going?"

"A mountain," I told her, my voice sounding powerful. Ascent would save us, the climb would purify us.

"We're in the middle of Kansas, dumb shit," Ann said.

That stumped me, but just for a second. "Haven't you ever heard of Indian Rock?" I asked.

"That little dirt mound," Ann said, shaking her head.

"It's steeper than it looks," I said.

Now, as my flip-flops flipped up leaf litter on my calves and as the branches of redbuds and young cottonwoods stung my face, I knew we had been weighed, measured, and found wanting. Proper cat care required more good sense than we had. I hugged Orvil tighter. The rough wood scraped over my bare arms. I could hear Ann's ragged breathing, and I could imagine her slick face. Her nose, so delicate, swelled and reddened when she cried. The long pods of a catalpa tree pointed down like daggers. I jogged to catch up with Ann, the coffin tucked football-like under my armpit.

Ann stopped. "I don't want to go back to school tomorrow," she said. "The students. They'll know something is wrong. They're like that, little hyenas. They can smell sorrow. Olga had a dog that died, and she told her class about it, just to explain why she was sad that day, and do you know what they did? One of them started chanting: 'Dead dog, dead. Dead dog, dead.' They all picked it up, then: 'Dead dog, dead!' I can't face that. These were second graders. Can you imagine a class full of twelve year olds to whom I'm supposed to teach triple meter?"

"Take a day," I told her. "Get a sub. We'll be hungover anyway." I sort of leaned toward her, rubbed her upper arm with mine. She wrapped her arms around me and said, "Maybe I will." It was awkward because I still held Orvil's box.

After more hard climbing, during which Ann fell and skinned her knee and the alcohol beat sharply in my forehead, my fingers aching until I thought I'd have to give up, just throw Orvil in the air and bury him wherever he landed, we reached the mountaintop, such as it was. The trees stood sparser—a few scraggly clumps of cedar. I thought at first that we must have climbed so high we'd reached the timberline. But when I looked down, I could clearly see my old Scout, its powdery yellow shining like a beacon, the crust of rust around the wheel wells still visible.

"There's the Scout," I told Ann, pointing.

She didn't look. She said, "Let's just get to digging. Where's the trowel?"

"I don't have it," I said.

"What?"

"I don't. You had it."

"No, I didn't."

I could have argued, but instead I said, "I must have lost it when I fell. I'm sorry. We'll have to use our hands." Ann sighed long and hard, like I was the stupidest individual she knew. I hated when she did this. She was too nice to say she thought I was a dumbass, but not nice enough to let things rest. That insult she'd been working on since I'd dropped Orvil now would be refined to diamond hardness. Still she held it on her tongue. Fine, I could wait.

We both scoured the ground for a good spot, and that's when we noticed that the mountain was not made of dirt, but rock. Native Kansas limestone. Not ideal for digging. The sunlight was weakening. Darkness would come soon.

"Well, shit," I said.

"Goddamn it, Hank," Ann said. "Why does everything have to be so fucking hard? You're the one who's supposed to be good at this."

"What?" I asked.

"Nature. Knowing what mountains are made of. I plan everything. Make sure we pay our bills on time, make grocery lists in my head, remember to feed the cat, because if I don't, who will?"

Purple rimmed her sunken eyes. I shivered. The sun was taking the warmth of the day with it. But I was actually relieved. Ann's words could have been so much worse. My first instinct was to tell her, guess what, I was exhausted too, just because I had an office job didn't mean I wasn't working hard, and she liked cooking so why shouldn't she shop because she knew what kind of shaved coconut to get and I sure as shit never did, she was the one who lost the trowel, and how the hell could anyone know that a mountain was stone on top just by looking at it from the ground. But if I did that, she'd start crying again, and she might dole out more blame. The dead cat seemed a likely place to start, and I couldn't stand to hear her say he was my fault. So instead, I said, "I know, you're right, I'm sorry. If you could just tell me what I can do."

That set her off. "No," she barked. "If I have to tell you what to do, I still have to think about it. It's still my problem. Can't you understand that? I thought you were going to take control. Now we've got a dead cat on our hands."

I set Orvil down and my brain started going, really trying to think about what she had said, to remember instances. Ann crying because I forgot to bring that little pillow she'd embroidered with our initials to the wedding, so we had nothing to strap the rings to, which had been my only job. Ann sighing copiously, scraping up stems and buds crusted to the counter from my attempts to dry ditchweed in the microwave so I could smoke it. Ann always letting Orvil in and out even though I sat by the door, could, in fact, reach the door handle if I had leaned ever so slightly to the left. Nearly every time she'd kick my chair, say hey, he's your cat, too, or ask, how could you not hear him?

I didn't know how. I really didn't. If it had been a commercial, or the seventh-inning stretch, maybe. But really? That was weak. Hearing was natural, like smelling. It just happened, except in my case. Shit. It was my own stupid fucking fault his bones got crushed, that his last seconds were pure terror. But she just nagged and nagged. She accused me of having no testicles. So help me, my balls twitched in pleasure when my fist met her cheekbone. And that lady, my wife, smiled. She actually smiled like, now I've got you, you piece of shit. And I've felt like a piece of shit ever since. But the problem wasn't her, it was me. Wife beater. Cat killer. Why couldn't she have divorced me rather than dangling me in limbo?

I hugged her, the coffin pressing against our chests. My arm clenched the sticky skin of her upper back, her damp tank top, her pointy shoulder blades. I wanted to hug her so hard we'd both forget we'd had a cat.

"I'm sorry," I whispered into her salty hair. She pushed me away. My legs got caught in a fallen tree limb, and I went down hard. She flew at me, scratching and hitting with fists half the size of mine. I used the coffin to fend her off, deflecting blows meant for my arms, my face, my eyes. She caught my hair and pulled. I struck her with the coffin just on the shoulder, not hard. She ripped the coffin away and jabbed right at my face with it and I shielded my nose with my forearms. The rough wood gashed my knuckles. I wriggled from side to side to escape the blows. "Stop," I yelled, "please stop."

She fell beside me and we both lay panting. I carefully wiped my arms and face on my shirt. We hated each other. But we were bound by this grief and by our hatred. Stronger, maybe, than love.

"You know what," I said, "the roots of those cedars yonder broke up the rock. I'll bet we could dig there okay."

"Great," Ann said.

I set Orvil under some bushes. We kicked a hollow in the gravel, and it was clear that she had said "great" unironically, not like great, another idea from dumbass, but like great, at last dumbass has a good idea, and maybe, just maybe in her head, she had replaced dumbass with my actual name and we had a chance. At last, we made the hole big enough so Orvil's casket could fit with ten inches of leeway between the top of the box and the top of the hole. It had taken forever. We refilled the gravel and set pinecones in a heart shape over his resting place. It felt sad, but good, too, like we had done right by Orvil in the end.

"Should we say something?" I asked. Ann nodded.

"Okay," I said. "Orvil was a good cat. His fur felt soft, and it was a nice color. He loved us, but not as much as he loved tuna. Remember how he'd tear into the kitchen as soon as he heard the can opener? He was very tidy. Every time he threw up, he'd find something to cover it with, like a plastic bag or my sock. And he spent so much time sharpening his claws, then he'd come stand on you and knead your stomach with them. He bit to show affection. I admired him for that. He was his own little man. The day I found him under the dumpster was one of the happiest days of my life."

"That was bad," Ann said.

I ignored her because I knew my words were true. As the twilight swallowed us, Ann grabbed my hand, and we looked at the place where we'd put him.

I worried we wouldn't reach the car before dark—I had neglected to bring a flashlight—but we made it in time. We gulped the rest of the brandy, and I threw the bottle deep into the tall grass.

As we bumped down the road toward a quieter house, Orvil began the long process of decay, his skin just starting to loosen from his flesh, which peeled from his bones. In time, my poison ivy blisters would pop, the scabs on my hands would heal, and night crawlers would gorge on Orvil's bloated form. Six months later, we would get a new cat, and my flawed carpentry job would make Orvil's box collapse. In another three months, Ann and I would celebrate our third wedding anniversary and most of Orvil's flesh would have rotted away. When we finally would decide screw it, let's get pregnant, the harder tissues—the cartilage, the tendons and ligaments, would have gone. And by the night we would conceive our baby girl, whom we'd name Miriam for the sweetness of its sound, nothing remained of Orvil but a small rib cage and a handful of orange fur.

Culvert Rising

FROM PAGE 2 OF THE Rural and Rising handbook, *Teaching Is Learning*:

> Regardless of when you first heard the Call to Teach, now you heed it,
> devoting your life to bright students who desperately need your help.
> Brave and noble, strong and full of passion, you answer the Call.

Nothing was wrong here. The body did as the mind wished, until the mind stopped wishing, and the body still did, which was the body's gift to the mind. Miriam's body guided her mother's old station wagon the last few miles down a one laner into a town of three thousand in western Kansas named Culvert, a scant five miles from the geodetic center of the country. The true interior. Behind the car, she pulled a U-Haul trailer with lots of yarn and a little furniture. The winter light caught the low crop (wheat? corn?) and it glowed emerald. A very few wind-bent cottonwoods rose berglike, their branches trembling. The landscape had the simple, artificial quality of a loop from an early video game, one that involved cross-country racing, maybe. A side-scroller. The horizon swung too low: more sky than anything, and blue blue blue. The deep dark blue of the far flat distance.

Here she was bound for the simple life on the prairie she'd always sought without knowing. The washed-out overalls, safety pinned on the sides, the faces like hatchets, like strip mines, open like wounds. The Germanic skin, red and blotched with sunspots. She'd been cast a thousand miles west from her East Coast college, past the small city in central Kansas where she grew up, all the way to Culvert, as sure as magnetic north. The magnetic west.

Western Kansas: where the hungry combine harvester chawed feet to the ankle if you took a wrong step. The hum and snarfle of the pig farm at night, the rattle of the metal pens in the scouring wind. The morning sun white in your eyes. Your teeth gritty. The slow stretch of time. The seasonal change of insects on your arms: gnat, tick, sweat bee, mosquito. Miriam felt whispers of these things, felt them in the icy breath of wind through the window, the glare on her forehead, though she didn't know them yet, and might never have words when she did.

Miriam's cell phone rang. She turned down the heater and the music—a mixtape by this young R&B singer in which he discusses how it might be better for him and his lady friend to be high for a certain sexual act—to answer.

The caller was her college roommate, Elizabeth, in her new postgrad apartment in Washington, D.C. She'd just started as a copywriter at an advertising firm in the city, which she referred to, maddeningly, metonymically, as the Beltway.

"I wanted to check on you," the roommate said, "moving out there all alone."

"You moved to D.C. all alone," Miriam said.

"Yes, but this is somewhere. Not terra incognita."

"How's Terence?" Miriam asked, figuring they had broken up.

"We broke up," the roommate sighed. "On New Year's, the bastard. I had the cutest dress, too. I looked like a mirror ball. And my eyeliner was just right but I cried it all off."

"That's too bad," Miriam said. "You'll find another guy on the Beltway."

"True enough!" Elizabeth said. "I just met this chef, kind of chubby and super cute in the face. He's got a rad dad bod. Never trust a skinny chef! Isn't that what they say?"

"What are you doing for fun out there?" Miriam asked.

"Drinking to excess. Just like old times. There's a girl from Mather House in my building. We're visiting every bar in a one-mile radius. We made a map and everything. A graph. We're averaging 3.7 bars per night."

Elizabeth kept bragging. Miriam rounded a corner and the landscape changed. A little muddy river flowed through the muddy banks, and trees flourished along the water's path. The sturdy bare limbs of the trees soothed her for a moment, but then she noticed a channel of twisted branches, bent trunks, and bare dirt that plowed through the trees' midst. A semi with a decal of an angry face over the grill sped past Miriam, bound for Colorado. A peeling billboard advertised Roundup-ready seed corn. You could spray the herbicide straight on your crops and they wouldn't die. A tornado. That's what had so torn up the land, had ripped right through that growing beautiful grove.

"Miriam? Hello?" Elizabeth said. "You should come back east. It's okay to have fun still, even after everything that happened. I know you don't like to talk about your parents."

"I'm not alone," Miriam said.

"Yeah. I guess. Be careful out there. Don't get chainsaw massacred," Elizabeth said. They hung up.

Miriam was touched by the call. Elizabeth worried because Miriam's father, Hank, had died during the first semester of their senior year, and then her mother, Ann, had died just a month before graduation. Miriam's father smoked a lot and ate fried potatoes at every meal (hash browns, chips, fries, repeat), so his passing was unsurprising.

Her mother, though, that was a blow. They'd both knit, and they were close-knit. They talked every day, about knitting and Miriam's romantic activities. It was Miriam's way of keeping herself honest. If she was unsure whether she should dally with some man, she'd let whether she could bear to tell her mother about him be her guide. After Miriam graduated in the spring, she and her mother had planned to open a yarn shop on a historic street in Miriam's hometown an hour north of Wichita. Her mother had just retired from teaching elementary school music, and they'd use the insurance money from her father's death for stock and fixtures. In between writing papers about the origins of Gothic literature in Scottish folk ballads, Miriam had shopped for alpaca, merino, and llama wool, point-of-sale software, display bins, and needles and notions.

One day, though, Miriam tried calling her mother's cell phone (she'd given a fellow with sweet dark eyes, a uniformed Israeli on furlough, a hand job behind some bushes outside a final club), but there was no answer. This struck Miriam as highly unusual, for her mother treated the cell phone like a normal phone, answering it every single time it rang, even if she was paying at a cash register or sitting in a waiting room or soaking in the bathtub.

That night a call came from Patty, her mother's neighbor. A FedEx delivery of a few pallets of worsted weight alpaca-silk had arrived at the house, and Miriam's mom didn't answer, so Patty signed for it.

"I didn't give it a thought, but then I did," Patty said. Miriam could barely understand Patty's voice through the crying. "Your mom was always so sweet. I'm so sorry. Clay will tell you."

There was a rustle as Patty passed the phone to Clay, her son, who'd been living with Patty now that his father, Jim, was gone. Clay had been Miriam's first boyfriend, back in high school. Miriam had also been the first person he'd come out to, after Miriam kept trying to push his hands onto her breasts and he kept pulling them away. Clay told her his father had found his porn and said he couldn't believe he'd raised a queer. Miriam told Clay she liked queers. They'd been friends ever since.

Clay said, "Hey Mir," and then he broke down, too. He passed the phone to his boyfriend, Damian, whom he'd described to Miriam when she ran into him last summer as "sex on a stick."

"Sorry," Damian said. "Nobody's holding up too good. I feel awful having to tell you this, but Patty found Ann. She tried to push open the front door but your mom's body was blocking it, I guess. Your mom fell down the stairs. She died. I'm so sorry. Clay told me all about you. I look forward to meeting you at the funeral."

"There was no smell," Patty said loudly in the background. "She wasn't warm, but there was no smell. Tell Miriam there was no smell."

"Do you have her cat, Fancy? He needs to be fed twice a day the special kidney food." Miriam was leaning against the window of her third-floor dorm room. She pressed her forehead hard against the thin old glass. Below her, a squirrel ran from one big tree to another and back, as though unsure which one held its nest. Miriam was eye level with the nest. She wished she could signal to the squirrel somehow that the first tree it had approached, the oak, was its home.

Damian said, "Actually, Miriam, Patty found Fancy, too. He was under your mother. Crushed, I guess."

wwww

Miriam found the exit for Culvert, just one for the whole place. There was no overpass, even. She pulled into town as the sun set, to a sign that read, "Welcome to Culvert: Where Pig Is King." On it a swine smiled coyly. Its eyes had been painted luminescent so they glinted in her headlights. The sign was studded with bullet holes, many from BBs, some from large-caliber bullets. Soon after the welcome sign, another sign read "Nat'l Headquarters, Scharf Batteries." This sign's lettering blurred at the edges, as though to indicate electric pulses. The small-town stench blew in through the open passenger-side window: stagnant water, dust, sweat, and cow . . . no, of course, pig manure. The windows of the low houses looked oily in the fading light, as if many noses had pressed on them. In one front yard a group of children had lashed a boy to a fire hydrant with a jump rope and they circled him whooping. When Miriam's car passed, they stopped to stare. She slowed to take a closer look. Their skin shone blue. It must have been the fading light that shaded the flesh so pallid, so cyan. She wondered if any of the children might be her students. They seemed somewhere between five and twelve years old. Miriam wasn't very good at telling. To be honest, she hadn't been around kids much. An only child herself, she hadn't preferred to fraternize with young people even when she was one. As she accelerated, the children seemed to chant: End of the road, end of the path.

Kids were the reason she was here now: to teach a third-grade class of twenty-eight students.

She'd gotten roped into Rural and Rising by Janet, a smooth-talking Korean American woman who wrangled kindergartners in the Mississippi Delta for three years. In November, a month before Miriam graduated (just one term late), Janet brought Miriam to an upscale Irish pub back in Boston and ordered Miriam a Jameson on the rocks. Miriam had seen an email on her house listserv about a January opening for a Rural and Rising position in a Kansas third-grade classroom. She knew the program was ultracompetitive, the purview of future high achievers on the national (liberal) political scene, but she thought maybe, due to the weird timing, she had a shot. Her grades had been quite good before her parents started dying.

"The basic thing," Janet said, after pitching the rich networking opportunities for R and R alums in the fields of education policy and social innovation, whatever that was, "is to maintain order. Make sure they don't hurt each other."

"Will they try?" Miriam asked.

"Will they try," Janet yelled, as if Miriam had made a joke. She asked Miriam why she wanted to teach for R and R, and Miriam spoke vaguely and unconvincingly about social justice and equitable education. Janet nodded as if Miriam had gotten the answers right. The truth was Miriam couldn't bear the notion of moving back to her childhood home in Salina once she graduated. To live among her dead parents' dead things. To sweep under the couch and turn up dead Fancy's little furry toys. To confront acquaintances in the grocery store, the doctor's office, the park, so eager to console her. Rural and Rising offered a clear plan, and it came with cheap rent. If Janet had been an abbess, Miriam would have donned a habit and taken vows. Sister (in need) of Charity. Usually, the R and R teachers descended on rural classrooms

in teams of two, but this was a special circumstance. Janet never speci-
fied the exact nature of the circumstance, but Miriam would soon find
out, she was sure. Culvert was three and a half hours west of Salina.
Miriam prayed that was far enough for a fresh start.

The front yards of the houses in Culvert were all neat, free of fallen
leaves, and strewn with lawn art like families of bunnies and deer.
There was an occasional Bible quotation on a white sign. Miriam
passed a sign a few doors down from her new rental house that read,
"The wages of sin is death." But that wasn't true. The wages of life is
death. Anyone might know that. And the plural "wages" with the sin-
gular "is" bothered her. Wage didn't work either. Finally, she spotted
the problem. The sign should have read: The wages of life are death.
The plural verb. What had she learned this year, if not that death was
always doggedly plural?

wMMw

From page 47 of *Teaching Is Learning*:

> You might find that the residents of your new town have different val-
> ues and traditions from your own. Remember too, though, that people
> are people wherever you are, and people are good!

She found her new house key on the kitchen counter, right where
the landlord, Karl Scharf, had promised. Few of the light bulbs worked,
but the place was large, certainly bigger than anything she could afford
in a city. Her new home had two bedrooms, a dishwasher, and a washer
and dryer in the basement, where she could hunker in case of a tornado. Central air. All for $425. The rooms smelled murky and citrusy,
like old cologne. She opened all the kitchen cabinets to see if someone
might have left a flashlight or a snack. She should have eaten at the
truck stop she'd seen in Colby that had billed itself the "Oasis on the
Plains," complete with Mylar palm trees in the lot.

In a drawer, she found a poorly printed nudie calendar from 1993
with the title *Takin' Care of Business*. Women in tight blazers and mini-
skirts mugged and thrust and draped across conference tables. The cal-

endar naturally fell open to September, a spread featuring a brunette with big black glasses, writing "2 + 2 = 4" on a chalkboard while hiking up her skirt. The teacher seemed to have forgotten her top. The front door of the house blew open. The wind whistled loudly. Miriam put the calendar back. She thought she'd latched the door.

She shut the door again and locked it, yearned for a deadbolt, and thought maybe she'd call her old roommate, Elizabeth, to let her know she got in safely, but her phone had no bars. She used her hair dryer to blow up the air mattress. She wished Fancy, at least, could be here. Fancy had been born in a barn, and Miriam's family adopted him as a kitten when Miriam was in the third grade. Her parents had lost another cat, Orvil, to a speeding pickup driven by Patty's husband, Jim, so Fancy was indoor only. Fancy never quite learned house manners, dragging his rear on the carpet and hissing if you got too near, but he loved Miriam. He'd jump on her lap and purr and lick and lick her arm until it was raw. He liked to sleep on her head like a coonskin cap.

Halfway through the night she was awoken by the smell of ozone. Thunder boomed. She was definitely back in the Midwest, where the weird weather might kick up a thunderstorm in January. She'd been dreaming she wore a helmet fashioned from big flashlight batteries that sizzled each time she approached a power line. The thunderstorm revealed the house's flaw: a skylight that dripped on the carpet. She tried to catch the water in a plastic bag, which was all she had, but the plastic magnified the sound of dripping.

In the morning she called the landlord, and he promised to hurry right over. She told him to let himself in. She had to get to school, and she suspected he might be the fan of Ms. September, which made her wary.

wwww

From page 544 of *Teaching Is Learning*:

> One of the great pleasures of small-town life is the warm sense of community. Don't be surprised when your new neighbors greet you with open arms, dropping off special casseroles or inviting you into their

homes for coffee or tea. You might soon find that your social calendar is so full that you barely have time for class prep!

There was a teachers' meeting in the lounge the morning after her arrival in town, only three days before the semester began. Due to her late hire, everything was rushed. Principal Kalt made Miriam stand at the front of the room while the other teachers, all ladies with close-cropped and tightly curled hair like fleecy nests, introduced themselves. They told Miriam how many years they had been teaching, which varied from twenty-seven to forty-one. They all wore black leggings. They reminded Miriam of molars, their legs the tooth's dead roots. Miriam had been told once, by a photography professor who wanted to fuck her, that she had "the gimlet gaze of an artist," which meant that he wanted to butter her up so he could fuck her.

"Meet my harem," Principal Kalt said, gesturing grandly. He was in his thirties, a full decade younger than any of the women, but somehow in charge. He had dark eyebrows and an impossibly thick mustache, curled up at the ends. The women leaned back in their seats, as if to avoid inclusion in the sweep of his arm. Miriam didn't like Principal Kalt, but she still smiled.

"So you're Mrs. Winkler's replacement," Mrs. Shelley said.

"I guess so," Miriam said. "Did she retire?"

"Fired," snapped Mrs. Sheldrake. The teachers all turned to Principal Kalt, who pursed his lips and gave a near-imperceptible shake of his head.

"You're cheaper than she was. You have no experience," Mrs. Sheldrake told her. Mrs. Sheldrake smiled as if she'd given a compliment, and Miriam smiled, too, as if she'd just received one. A true midwestern impasse: everybody was smiling but nobody meant it.

"Experience comes in many forms," Miriam said. This wasn't her first time in a teachers' lounge. Her mother had taught grade school music until she took early retirement, after all. The lounge walls at Miriam's mother's elementary school had been covered with students' drawings and funny sayings and cartoons showing endlessly patient teachers and comically inept pupils. The walls in this lounge were bare.

90

After the meeting, Principal Kalt drew her aside. The wetness of his palm soaked her sleeve to her skin.

"Don't you worry about those ladies. They'll come around. And if they don't, R and R has already promised that there are plenty more young people where you came from," he said.

"Okay," Miriam said. She pretended to have to scratch her thigh, so she could free her arm from his grasp. "Mrs. Winkler wasn't really fired so I could replace her, was she?"

Principal Kalt sucked air between his long teeth. "You know these ladies aren't like you and I. They don't come from anywhere," Principal Kalt said. "I'm from Dodge City. Before this I was a line manager at Scharf Batteries. Got the scars to prove it." He unbuttoned his dress shirt at the collar to show her his shoulder, where the skin was pocked with raised pink blotches. "Different job, same shit, I like to say."

"I don't seem to be making friends," she said.

"Well, you've made one," he said, his mustache dancing.

Mr. Kalt showed Miriam to her classroom, a beige box with a chalkboard at the front, windows along one side, and a coat closet on the other side. At the back of the room was a long counter, sink, and supply closet, and at the front of the room was Miriam's desk, a wide oak boat with a few items stacked on top. "This is just the old teacher's garbage," Mr. Kalt said, sliding them into a gray metal trash can.

After he left, Miriam fished everything back out: a tangled dream catcher, a geode slice with a stuck-on nameplate that read "Mrs. Winkler," a little gold Buddha, and a rainbow poster of a woman seated in lotus position with her chakras labeled. Miriam put the Buddha and the geode back in the desk drawer and returned everything else to the trash.

She wiped down the desks and counter with a scratchy brown paper towel and practiced writing her name in cursive on the board. She discovered art materials in her supply closet and spent a few happy hours designing the bulletin board recommended in *Teaching Is Learning*. It featured a tadpole named Hal who could only change into a frog when multiplicands were paired with their correct product.

She'd picked up a copy of the Dodge City newspaper on her way into town the previous day and had been horrified and intrigued by an article about the deformed frogs that area residents had been finding in their yards: legs sprung from frogs' heads and sides and even from other legs. The article had quoted a Culvert pig farmer: "We have no idea what might cause it. Just God's will, I guess."

Miriam considered adding a few extra limbs to Hal for verisimilitude, but figured the children were too young to reckon with mutation.

wWm

From page 15 of *Teaching Is Learning*:

> The most powerful aspect of teaching is the way your own thoughts and concerns are subsumed by your students' needs. Rural and Rising teachers give of themselves fully, and you are all such bright, dynamic young individuals that you have quite a bit to give.

Miriam pulled up to the post office. She was feeling satisfied about how much she'd accomplished less than fifteen hours after arriving in a whole new town. Here she was, with her hair washed and styled, makeup applied—a cat eye nearly symmetrical—black skirt, silk shirt, black mules, casual but still nice, picking up her boxes of books and clothes and household sundries she'd quite responsibly mailed to herself from college, ready to start a job she had been hired to do! And what good work, helping the economically and geographically disadvantaged! To give back some of what she'd taken by dint of the good luck of a middle-class birth! The goal of R and R, as far as Miriam could tell, was to save the children of the rural poor from their hardscrabble fates by educating them, sending the smart ones to cities for college and more lucrative and meaningful work.

What the other teachers said about her predecessor being fired to make room for new blood gave her pause, but then she remembered she was young, and all that implied: energy, a lack of experience in failure, and good skin. The world was hard. Old people got chewed up, some well before their time. Only the young were agile enough to dodge the reaper's swing. A farm metaphor. Already she'd acclimated.

The postal clerk wore what looked like Miriam's handknit purple mohair sweater. He insisted her boxes hadn't arrived. He told her, "Sometimes that happens. Can't always count on the mail."

Had he made a joke? He didn't smile. He was very thin, with downy white hair and invisible eyebrows, and his uniform pants were cinched tight with a snakeskin belt that resembled one that Miriam wore with her magenta pencil skirt. His face was scarred like the principal's shoulder: marked with pink, shiny skin all across the forehead and down the nose to the chin. The "T zone," her beauty magazines called this area. They had tips for deoiling it but never for concealing acid burns.

When he noticed her staring at him, he collapsed dramatically across the counter, sending a pile of priority envelopes flying. She hadn't seen her father dead on his desk, but she'd pictured it plenty, and the postal employee did it just like she'd imagined, down to the protruding tongue.

He sat back up and grinned. "Scharf stole my youth! Filled some AAs too full and the inevitable happened. They had to peel my nose off the belt. I did get some bucks under the table for my troubles. Now I only work fifteen hours a week." He began restacking envelopes. He used her Norton Critical Edition of *Jane Eyre* to weigh down the piles. If he ever cared to turn to page 110, he'd see her note in pink pen: "Rochester is such a self-pleased dickface."

Back in her car, she lowered her head onto the steering wheel and wept so hard she knocked her head into the horn. She left it there. The long honk soothed her. So she had dragged those boxes a half-mile from her dorm to the post office using a dolly with two flats. So once she'd arrived at the Cambridge post office she'd learned it'd cost $191.72 to mail the boxes, and she'd paid it, despite the fact that her bank account had $78.34. If the R and R folks hadn't advanced her half her first month's check, she wouldn't have had a rental deposit. She was broke. Skint, as a British dude who'd gone down on her in a sushi restaurant bathroom and then fucked her against the towel dispenser used to say.

She wiped away the mascara from her cheeks and drove to her new house. Maybe the postal clerk desperately needed her sweater because minimum wage in the county was something ridiculous like $4.62 an hour. Perhaps he'd read *Jane Eyre* and he, an orphan himself, would relate to Jane's conflicting desires for family and for independence and would at last make peace with the roiling uncertainty that arose from his liminal place in the world. Most likely, Miriam decided as she turned onto her street, he'd pawn what he could for a handle of some terrible corn-based alcohol that'd gradually melt his esophagus.

The U-Haul trailer's door gaped open in her driveway, the padlock hanging unlatched on the hasp. Robbed! She started crying again, but when she got inside, she found that someone (her landlord?) had patched the ceiling with a big piece of plywood, aimed an industrial fan at the wet spot on the carpet, and arranged all the yarn from the U-Haul in piles by color family. She sunk into green and expected to cry more but instead she laughed.

wmmm

From page 4 of *Teaching Is Learning*:

> New teachers frequently remark on the humor of Rural and Rising's nickname, R and R. Rest and relaxation is the last thing you'll get in our challenging program. As our founder Melody O'Dell always said, "Wasted hours add up to wasted years, which, before you know it, add up to a wasted life."

Miriam didn't sleep much the night before her first day of class. Cold wind rushed through cracks where doors and windows met walls, despite her efforts to plug the fissures with yarn. She kept hearing little scratching sounds at her bedroom window. She put on her robe and crept outside with a flashlight. Miriam had expected a tree limb or, at worst, a raccoon, but a man hunched in the bushes.

"What the fuck do you want?" Miriam said. The man didn't move, so she started yelling. "What? What?" The whats came out longer and shriller, more like screams.

He stayed so still that she thought he might be dead. She got close and eased her foot forward to nudge the body with her toe, but he sat straight up. He wore black shorts, a black sweatshirt, black tennis shoes, and black socks pulled way up on his calves. He wasn't too much older than her.

"Oh, fuck!" Miriam said.

"Your momma know you talk like that?" he said.

"Who the hell are you?"

"I'm Karl Scharf. Your landlord. The wind was howling so bad, I figured I'd better come and check the roof."

"It's fine."

"You sure?" he asked. "You don't want me to come in, take a look? You here all alone like this." He smiled, showing very long white teeth. He looked a little like Wario to Principal Kalt's Mario. Or vice versa. Karl didn't have a mustache, though. Something she'd noticed and tried not to draw any conclusions about: lots of folks in town looked the same.

"Why were you kneeling if you wanted to look at the roof?" Miriam asked.

"Oh, I thought I saw a shingle fall off. Back that way. Way back. All right, then." He stretched his legs out and heaved himself up stiffly, as if he'd been squatting a long time. "Whew. A little nippy tonight. You heard my last name?"

"Scharf?"

He nodded. "You know what that means around here?"

Sure, she'd seen that sign on the way into town, as well as on the biggest building in town, or rather, the longest and widest, a dismal gray stretch of loading docks and small high windows.

"I've seen two people already with awful burns," Miriam said.

He laughed, "Aw, that was an issue with a new agitator. The inverter didn't regulate the mixing speed too hot and sulfuric acid jetted up and stung a few folks."

"How many?"

"Oh, about forty-five. You let me know if you'd ever care for a private tour of the line."

"That must have been quite a lawsuit," Miriam said.

"Nah," Karl said. "We just said sorry to all, paid their medical bills, and gave 'em some free land by the pig farm."

He gave her a jaunty honk as he drove away in his pickup.

Miriam went back inside and locked the door behind her. She yearned for a deadbolt. She checked each window. The bedroom window didn't latch right so she nailed it shut. She sat in bed waiting for the light to come in the east, wishing her cell phone could get reception, wondering, even if it worked, who in the world she might call.

wwww

From page 220 of *Teaching Is Learning*:

> Inevitably, you'll have a student who misbehaves in your classroom. The important thing to remember in these situations is that you must keep calm. You've got a whole team of administrators behind you, not to mention the empathetic and wise input more experienced fellow teachers can provide. You should never feel alone in your classroom.

Miriam, or Miss Green, as she would be known to her students, stepped from the cracked curb toward her eighteenth annual first day of school. Twentieth if she counted the two years at Creative Corners Preschool, where she'd been so jealous of the student with the sixteen-color crayon box that included pink. Miriam had made friends with the other little girl, and later the other little girl gave her the pink crayon. Miriam always excelled in circumscribed situations. Top scorer in calculus, best science project, junior high through senior class president. She imagined Culvert would offer more of the same opportunities.

Her heels kept catching in the gravel, wobbling her ankles. She wanted to walk faster, but she remembered her mother's old saying: Slow and steady wins the race. With her tweed skirt and fitted black silk tank, she looked like a true young professional. She carried the R and R tote bag proudly—her badge, for there was a new sheriff in town.

Its very presence suggested that she, this twenty-two year old, had any right to impart wisdom to twenty-eight eight year olds, who would much rather be chewing on their fingers or, oh, whatever else children of that age liked to do. The R and R manual hadn't gotten into much detail, and to be frank, she'd always avoided small children. She didn't like their busy hands and dripping noses.

The wakeful night had left Miriam's brain buzzy and tender, so she said supportive things to herself aloud ("They're just little people!" and "Eight hours and you can nap!"), which explained why she didn't hear the rumbling. As she turned, she saw a shiny black pickup truck coming fast, one headlight dangling like a popped-out eyeball. She turned her ankle and slipped out of her shoe as she scrambled to the curb. The truck braked sharply and its front tire crushed her lost shoe.

"Get along now!" barked a voice, which must have belonged to the owner of the sunburned arm protruding from the tinted window. Miriam watched as three children with rattails piled out and ran across the schoolyard. Their skin had a blue cast, as if they'd swum in a winter lake. The middle child wore glasses with a safety strap. The truck peeled away. Miriam retrieved her shoe. The heel had snapped in two. She stuffed the ruined shoe and bit of heel in her satchel and limped into the building. The guy probably couldn't even see her from so high in that cab. She'd borrowed her dad's ancient Scout for a week once when her car was in the shop, and she noticed how easy it seemed to run over small obstacles like traffic cones or curbs or pedestrians. The fraternity of truck drivers had surprised her, too—nary a Silverado passed without a wave or nod. When her parents had died, she'd considered keeping the Scout rather than the station wagon, but her father had smoked in the Scout and the stench of Salem Ultra Light 100s was too much. Her mother's station wagon smelled only of car.

Miriam had noticed nice vehicles tooling around town. The houses were tiny, well-maintained but aging ranches, built in the late forties and fifties after men returned from World War II. But the trucks were all late model, extended cab, leather interior, super-duty, a whole different species from Miriam's vehicle. Though R and R offered its services only to economically depressed communities, Miriam received mixed signals about Culvert. On one hand, you had to go a hundred miles for soymilk; on the other, people drove $60,000 pickup trucks. Priorities differed. That was a lesson of travel.

In her classroom, Miriam crafted a splint for the broken heel from a Popsicle stick and Scotch tape, but when she stood, the tape ripped and she twisted her ankle. Glue might work better, but all she had was the white stuff that took forever to dry. She seemed to remember a lost and found box in the teachers' lounge. Maybe it had shoes. Adults didn't lose shoes, but some of the children seemed quite large.

She hobbled down the hall. The floor felt cool and gritty under her bare foot. Children's shrill voices floated from the cafeteria. Her heart thumped. The job seemed real suddenly. Teaching was a fine thing to say she was doing, the humanitarian impulse, but to actually walk into a classroom day after day, facing down those small shiny eyes? Anything in a big enough group was terrifying. Clouds. Locusts. Kids.

The teachers' lounge was occupied by Mrs. Sheldrake and another teacher whose name she didn't know. She should have known it, because this teacher also taught third grade, but when she met people lately, she'd get so nervous about saying her own name that she'd forget to listen, and now it was too late.

Mrs. Sheldrake smiled and shifted her body toward Miriam with the same expansive satisfaction with which Fancy used to regard a low-crawling spider.

"I wonder what poor Mrs. Winkler is doing right now? Probably clipping coupons, trying to figure out how she can stretch this week's meat purchase," Mrs. Sheldrake said. "It's a blessing that her husband passed all those years ago. She always wanted children, but her womb was barren, bless her, so she devoted her life to teaching instead." She looked at Miriam like she expected an apology.

"I'm just in search of a shoe. Mine got driven over," Miriam said.

"I thought that was the style among young people," the other teacher said. "Like the boys with the backward overalls."

"I don't know about that," Miriam said.

"You probably shouldn't steal from the lost and found box," Mrs. Sheldrake said.

"I'm borrowing."

"You probably shouldn't borrow what isn't yours without asking. That's what I tell my first graders."

Inside the box was a grimy gray sneaker, several sizes too large, for the wrong foot. It smelled of yeasty cheese. She dropped the sneaker back down among the torn hoodies and house keys on string.

Mr. Kalt visited the lounge to mention to the three of them that his office door was always open (except when it was closed, of course). A principal, he reminded them, was a prince who was also a PAL. That last bit was important, he emphasized. He paused for laughs. No one laughed but Miriam, who did her fake laugh, which sounded like she was choking. The other third-grade teacher pounded her on the back, a human touch that made Miriam feel hideously, shamefully grateful.

After Mr. Kalt left, the other third-grade teacher asked to look at Miriam's roll sheet. Neither the other third-grade teacher nor Mrs. Sheldrake knew any of Miriam's students themselves, but they had some thoughts based on last names. The Zweigs were all dumb as stumps, and to be a Pappenheim was to possess an equine head, always red around the nostrils. When the Jungnickels sweated, it smelled like rotting leaves.

"Watch the anger with those Jungnickels," Mrs. Sheldrake said. "A tight-wound bunch."

⁓⁓⁓

From page 341 of *Teaching Is Learning*:

> You might be feeling apprehensive or even downright scared today, your first day of class, but keep in mind, your students are eager to see you as their mentor and friend. This is one of the greatest moments for any Rural and Rising teacher, when you seize control of a classroom and start shaping eager young minds. Go get 'em!

Back in her classroom, Miriam dumped the contents of the R and R satchel onto her desk. She grabbed her Rising reader covered with highlighting and notes for leading discussions (example: Why did

Paulie tell his sister that he didn't like her drawing of the coyote?). She had read through the story "A Coyote for Sarah" nigh on nine times now, had, in fact, fallen asleep with it open on her stomach last night, before Karl's lurking woke her. So much had gone so wrong in her life lately that she wanted to get this one small thing, this first day, right. If she prepared enough, reviewed her materials and her lesson plan, she might stave off every poor outcome.

The satchel was nine by twelve inches, with the long side running vertically. It fit eight-and-a-half-by-eleven-size papers snugly. A small white paper tag sewn into an inside seam read "Made in Malaysia." A Malaysian person had crafted this bag just so Miriam could march into the classroom and look like a pro. Maybe an eight year old, just like the ones she'd instruct today. "Rural and Rising" was screen printed on one side in a blocky, sans serif font. R and R did not condone anything frivolous, such as Garamond or Caslon or, lord forbid, Bookman Old Style.

She felt a little bad about mustering so little of the colonizer's zeal for her students. A hidden finger of doubt pressed right on her spine wouldn't allow her to say, "I come from a more sophisticated place, and thus, I know better how you benighted people should live. Let me save you."

Something about this failed paternalism reminded her of a past happy scene. One morning when Miriam was six, her father didn't have to work, and both of her parents had walked her to school. She held their hands and every few steps she'd swing on their arms. Miriam felt so light. At last her mother had told her to stop because it made her arm hurt. "You're just a big lug these days," her mother said, smiling. "Lug, lug, lug," Miriam said, over and over, until it sounded like love. They all smiled. There was no one to shepherd her gently through life anymore, as she was expected to do now, with these youngsters.

She lined up the Rising reader on her desk, parallel with the edge. She reviewed page 14, which introduced the tricky vocabulary word "carnivore." She picked up the book and posed with it against her chest like Laura did with her doll on the cover of *Little House in the Big Woods*. Now, those Ingallses didn't struggle with right and wrong when it came to settling a farmstead on Native American lands. Laura's

Ma hated the Native Americans, but Pa had said, "They are perfectly friendly." She cleared her throat and cleared it again and vowed to be like Pa among these Culvert folks, descendants, perhaps, of the Ingalls family themselves. Was Ingalls a German name? She didn't notice any Native American names on her roster.

The students rushed in.

Miriam stood at the front of her class, feet just over shoulder-width apart, owning the space, as R and R had taught her. Twenty-eight third graders squirmed below her, though it felt like more, not tens but hundreds, each with an icy blue-eyed gaze. The similarity of the children's appearances suggested that recent non-European immigration to Culvert was uncommon. The ceiling tiles zoomed away and Miriam had to grab hold of the desk to steady herself. She wished she were in the middle of the ocean, an abandoned salt mine—anywhere but this classroom. If she could just dissolve to liquid and squirt under the door and down the hall and out the main door across the sidewalk and into the soil of the schoolyard, that'd suit her fine.

"Hi, welcome to school. I'm Miss Green, and I'll be your teacher this year," she forced herself to say. Her voice had the high, quavery quality that a therapist she'd briefly seen after her folks' passing had always remarked on. The therapist seemed to hate women, or at least femininity, Miriam had decided, before she'd abandoned her sessions. The therapist had a little wicker tea strainer that fit over his cup, and he'd always pack the loose tea down with his thumb, which made the strainer squeak vexingly. Miriam could only imagine what fungi and bacteria that strainer harbored.

Two students took turns slapping each other hard across the face.

"Hey!" Miriam shouted, "Cut it out."

The students blinked up at her, startled. Several students had abandoned their desks to roam to the windows, where they peered out vacantly at the tetherball pole. Others stood at the chalkboard, slashing it with chalk. She found a student in the cupboard under the sink shaking a pile of Comet into her hand. "What are you going to do with that?" Miriam asked. The student raised the little mound of powder to her mouth and inched out her tongue. "No!" Miriam said. "Drop it!"

The student obeyed. They listened to her when she told them to stop, but they couldn't seem to stay still. It felt like a game of red light, green light, except instead of sneaking toward her when she looked away, they fled. At last ten thirty arrived, and they all obeyed when she told them to line up for recess.

When she and the kids returned, her classroom had changed. Decorations Miriam had hung so lovingly the week before class—Lopi the American Bison and the Multiplication Tadpole—lay on the floor in tatters. Some students laughed nervously as Miriam examined the damage; others sat stone-faced, their thighs jouncing under the desks. Miriam wasn't sure which students she suspected more. R and R had taught her that she should never be flustered in front of the students. She took a deep breath and asked the students to help her clean up the mess. They did with no complaints.

uMm

From page 587 of *Teaching Is Learning*:

> Frequently, R and R teachers give of themselves so much that they get all worn out. To stave off burnout, be sure to make time for yourself. Even a few minutes a day doing an activity you enjoy like knitting or reading can help get your batteries recharged.

After that first day of teaching, Miriam went to the convenience store to pick up dinner. The store seemed to specialize in off-brand mac and cheese and meats in cans. The nearest lettuce was in Dodge City. As she waited in line with her tinned peaches and tub of cottage cheese, she pondered her students' diets. No wonder they couldn't attend to her lessons or recall things she'd said mere minutes before. Lack of nutrition. Boys and girls didn't thrive by Ho Hos and fried bologna alone. Here, soybeans flourished, but the crop fed the pigs. How could the children be expected to concentrate on book learning when their bodies pulsed with sugar and partially hydrogenated oils?

The man in front of her in line, who wore Key Imperial bib overalls and was scratching an angry patch of skin above his wrist, paid for his nacho pack and night crawlers, and Miriam unloaded her food onto the counter. The clerk, who could have been the postman's twin, said the total was $5.67 and held out his palm.

Miriam ran her fingers through the empty mouth of her wallet. There'd been a twenty there this morning. She'd stowed her purse in the unlocked supply closet, despite other teachers' warnings to leave valuables locked in her car trunk. Her lipstick would have frozen in the cold. "Where's the closest ATM?" she asked.

"There are no ATM machines in Culvert," he told her. "Bank's closed, too."

"Oh dear. Credit card?"

"Nope."

"Well, all right. Do you people, can I put something on a tab of some sort and pay later, when the banks open?"

"Nope, no credit unless we know you." He smiled. "Checks, either."

"But I live here now. I teach third grade."

"Yeah, I know."

"Okay." Miriam left the basket on the counter and walked out. After she reached her car, she realized it had been rude to leave the basket. She had probably angered the only food purveyor for miles. He didn't look angry. Well, he hadn't looked unhelpful, either. Did his behavior count as xenophobia if she hailed from the other side of the state? And further, where were all the people of color? No one but Mr. Kalt and Karl Scharf had dark hair. Her head ached and her stomach hurt. The smell of the pigs had permeated her car upholstery, her clothing. She hadn't had a normal bowel movement in a week and a half. She'd lost three pounds already.

She drove east to try to call someone, anyone. She passed her small rental home, the other small homes owned by the citizens outright, the battery factory, the hog pens and waste lagoons around which turkey buzzards circled, the backside of the welcome sign, on which was spray-painted "go away," twenty miles until the cell phone reception kicked in. She called Janet.

"I expected the place to be a little sad, a little bleak," Miriam told Janet. Between Miriam's voice, pitched high and wispy, and the limited reception, Janet said she could barely hear. Miriam tried to talk from deep in her churning belly so her voice would carry across the miles. "I don't think they want me here. The students. The way they look at me sometimes, with their eyes all narrowed, then nod at each other and smile. They know too much. It isn't right."

"Miriam, I think you're giving these kids too much credit. They're eight."

"They stole from me. They stole my grocery money."

"They need help, Miriam. They live in poverty. It's a cycle. That's why you're there. You have the chance to really save some of these kids. Lift them up."

"Yeah," Miriam said. They were at cross-purposes because Janet believed in Miriam's ability to effect change. The conversation could drag on for an hour at this rate. She wanted to get to Dodge City, use the ATM and get groceries, and lock herself in with a chair against the front door before it got dark and Karl came a-calling.

"My landlord's a perv," Miriam said.

"You know, we don't like to send teachers out to a school alone. Usually they're in teams of two. But you are such a strong applicant—"

"You thought I could handle it." This was how Janet had lured Miriam in the first place, this flattery.

"You can handle it. Have the students do some work in small groups. Small groups can make them more manageable. And lock your doors and windows."

Miriam listened to her voicemails. One was from an angry yarn purveyor eager to secure payment from her mother, and the other was from her old roommate, Elizabeth. The yarn purveyor threatened to pursue legal action. Good luck when her mother didn't even exist anymore. You're suing a corpse! A shade! A pile of charred bone in a cardboard box from the crematory that Miriam still couldn't bear to open. Now don't you feel terrible? Miriam would ask. Terrible. Her roommate wanted to know if Miriam had heard that one of their classmates, whom they'd last run into during spring break at a club in the Bahamas with machine-gun-toting bouncers and a swimming pool in the mid-

dle of the dance floor, had gotten pregnant. "That dumb bitch!" Elizabeth had crowed. "I'll bet the dad is one of those random dudes from
Clemson she was grinding on. Way to waste your life."

Miriam considered calling her old roommate, who most probably
really did love her and wish her the best, but she couldn't face Elizabeth, even over the phone. If she hit on sympathetic ears, she might
blurt out what a mistake she'd made, how nothing she'd done had been
right, not for a long time.

₩₩₩

From page 162 of *Teaching Is Learning*:

> Sometimes rowdy minds and busy hands can overwhelm the most as-
> sured and confident instructor. Luckily, an easy fix is at your fingertips:
> have the students do work in small groups. Small groups can make your
> classes more manageable.

Something odd happened on the second day of class. The lessons
started smoothly. She caught a few students nodding along. She threw
in an impromptu minilesson, asking if the students knew why we
said "ATM" rather than "ATM machine." "Because it's an initialism.
Saying 'ATM machine' was just silly, because 'machine' was already
right there in the word. It would be like saying 'automatic teller machine machine.'" Pause for laughs. None forthcoming. A student in the
first row raised her hand and asked, "What's an ATM machine?" Miriam told her. The students perked up at the mention of a machine that
dispensed money, but they lost interest when they found it was just
money you already had.

Miriam divided the students into groups as Janet and *TIL* recommended. She gave each group member a task: facilitator, recorder,
summarizer, and presenter. The students didn't know what any of
these words meant. Miriam tried to explain, but it took too long, and
the student with the strap around his glasses, Jericho Jungnickel, took
the strap off and whipped it at a girl, who started crying. While Miriam

tried to comfort the girl, another student pulled volumes of *World Book Encyclopedia* from the low shelf under the windows and stacked them on her desk in piles of varying height to create primitive stairs. The student climbed the pile and jumped to catch at a hanging cord that controlled the fan. She missed and landed on another student, sending both of them down in a thrashing, screaming pile. An awful smell rose from the back of the room, where a student had vomited and hidden the small wet pile with the beanbag chair. "And now it's time for lunch," Miriam announced.

The lock on the classroom door held during lunch and recess. At the end of the day, as she gathered up her teacherly things in her R and R satchel—half-finished worksheets, pens, the *Rural Reader*—she saw something black on the surface of Cy's desk in the back of the class. Cy was a larger student, tall and soft-bodied. One of his eyes had an opalescent gray cast so he'd turn his head to line up his good eye when he really wanted to see you. She approached the desk and looked down. Hundreds of circles drawn with a pencil covered the desk. Each circle's size and shape varied. They seemed to swirl together. It was beautiful, like a close-up of a mass of feathers or cells under a microscope. She took a picture with her phone before she rubbed the image away with some spit on her palm.

wmm

From page 498 of *Teaching Is Learning*:

> Sometimes you might find that students forget to show the same respect to you as other, older teachers. If this happens, you might need to gently remind them that you are still the one with authority. One great way to do this is with a freewriting exercise. The topic: What are some ways I can show my teacher how much I value him/her/them?

Seventeen of Miriam's twenty-eight students gripped their pencils in their fists, like cave people. Nine of Miriam's students shouted "No!" each time she asked a question. Two students had never said anything in class except "No." One student who wore gray sweatpants every day had a flap of skin that attached the tip of his tongue to the bottom of his mouth. He might not have been saying "No." It was hard to judge.

All of the students had slow reaction times. She expected them to be much quicker than she was, but instead they were like little potheads, laughing at jokes minutes too late, blinking up blankly when she posed even the simplest of yes or no questions (Do you like to eat apples? Do you have a pet?). Six students had already been excused to the nurse's office due to stomachaches. Miriam was sure they were malingering, but then she spoke with the nurse, who told her this was frequent. "I buy Tums in megapacks," she said, showing off a barrel of chalky tablets. When Miriam asked her why the children's stomachs pained them, she'd shrugged. "Maybe the teachers are giving them too much homework? Maybe children these days don't have the strong constitutions of their parents?" The question Miriam had wanted to ask: In what ways might these children be like mutant frogs?

Miriam had believed that the strange blue cast on the children's skin was caused by the overhead fluorescents, but then she noticed that the color remained even at recess, even in the lunchroom. A smaller student named Tuxton was struggling to wash his hands after he'd pet the class turtle so Miriam helped him, lathering and lathering all up his arms, wondering if the blue might somehow wash down the drain. She scrubbed too hard with the rough paper towels, and Tuxton yelped and writhed away. He kept his distance from her after that.

At recess, the children played strange games where they dug pits in the softball field and buried beer cans from the schoolyard fence, where the older kids had thrown them out of trucks. They'd get the holes half-started only to wander away to the monkey bars.

Miriam had herself been an intense child. She fixed on an activity and pursued it to its logical conclusion—she marbled paper using a cheap watercolor set, read every book by an author she liked, dug for clay in the backyard to mold sculptures for her mother to bake in the oven. She had trouble relating to this group of nondoers. It was as though their creative capacity had withered like an unpollinated bud.

From page 220 of *Teaching Is Learning*:

> Inevitably, you'll have a student who misbehaves in your classroom.
> The important thing to remember in these situations is that you must
> keep calm. You've got a whole team of administrators behind you, not
> to mention the empathetic and wise input that more experienced fel-
> low teachers can provide. You should never feel alone in your classroom.

Miriam discovered she had a true ally in Principal Kalt. She'd find
herself in his office after school, at least a few times a week. She sat in
one of the two armchairs for beleaguered parents, and he started out in
his desk chair but eventually moved to the other comfy chair near her.
His office was the only one with working climate control. The other
rooms' radiators pumped out heat, so Miriam would enter Kalt's office
with sweat dripping down her back, and after a few minutes of evap-
oration, her skin would be cool and dry. They drank tea at first, then
ouzo.

"Where do you get ouzo in Culvert?" Miriam asked.

"You can get most things you want if you know where to look," he
said. Miriam pulled her blouse higher up her neck.

Initially, Miriam had formulated a vague plan to find an older, female teacher to take her under her wing, but so far the other women
had stonewalled her. She'd even tried bringing up her passion for knitting and all the yarn she had to share—good merino and cotton, not
the acrylic garbage they sold at craft stores—but the other teachers
liked the acrylic garbage. It was durable.

So Principal Kalt was all she had and she tried to be grateful.

She asked him all her burning questions: "Why are the students so
slow and incurious?"

"Hey now," he said. "Don't disparage them just 'cause they aren't
scholars. We need people to man the line at the factory, too. Plenty of
folks are happy to work and go home."

"Why does everyone have such nice trucks?"

"We're a two-company town, Miriam. You know that," he said, slapping her leg, which she uncrossed to remove from his reach. "And

Scharf Industries and Durftig Farms take such good care of us. Our families. They're like loving parents."

"You're telling me factory jobs here pay enough for those trucks?"

"I am. When you commit to making a quality product, using good American labor, you can charge more for that product and pay the people who make it well."

"Why is everyone here white?"

Principal Kalt looked off over Miriam's shoulder. "Nobody else has chosen to move in. We keep ourselves to ourselves."

"But I moved here," Miriam said.

"You're okay, though. You aren't looking to rock the boat."

Miriam hadn't even thought about rocking the boat until he pointed out the possibility. She wondered how she might make some waves. Lobby for higher teacher salaries? Petition for better access to free and reduced-price student lunches? More fresh fruits and vegetables? A study of the effects of breathing the pungent gases from the hog lagoons day in and day out? A test of the drinking water for contaminants?

In class earlier that day, she'd had three students nod off and another two roll on the floor cupping their stomachs and moaning.

⁓⁓⁓

The other teachers, most likely led by Mrs. Sheldrake, still refused to speak with Miriam. Whenever Miriam would try to sit with them at lunch and make conversation, they'd turn their bodies away from her or talk to each other over her head. She hadn't been treated that way her first time in elementary school. She decided to take her little tray into the library, where she could eat in silence. The librarian dropped a whole stack of DVD cases when Miriam cracked open the library door.

"Oh! What do you want?" the librarian asked. She wore cheetah-print glasses on a beaded chain, and her silvery-brown hair was carefully coiffed into a duckbill over her forehead. She'd never need a visor.

"I just want somewhere to eat. I teach here," Miriam said. Without a word, the librarian walked out. Miriam never saw her again. Miriam pictured the librarian sitting in a stall in the girls' restroom until Miriam left her space, but she knew it was much more likely that the woman just hung out with the other teachers in the lunchroom, gossiping about the weird young teacher, half-girl, half-woman, who insisted on eating lunch in the library.

Much of the library's holdings consisted of DVDs on various educational topics, but there were still some books. Miriam read a book about badminton. She read one about child detectives who lived in a covered wagon. She read one about May Day, which was a Germanic pagan celebration in which merrymakers erected a tall pole, a May Pole, that they wrapped with ribbons. The May Pole represented the permeability of the boundary between the earth and the heavens. Certain spots in the world blurred the real and unreal, living and dead. The axis mundi, for one, the center of the world, around which everything spun. For some cultures, the axis mundi was the tallest mountain, a vertical spit soaring to the sky, so one who stood atop it might commune with the dirt below and the heavens above, a human lightning rod for the charge of energy from whatever might wait just on the other side of the visible world, the body a suture for the split between the earthly and cosmic. She longed to find a high spot and camp out until she received a transmission from beyond. She yearned to build herself a May Pole and use it to call out to her departed beloveds. She picked up a book about a dog who was somehow able to play the banjo with his paws and teeth, but she set it down. She started to cry. She gasped and honked. She wiped the tears off her face with the Peter Pan collar of her blouse.

When Miriam was her students' age, her and her mother's favorite holiday was May Day. They had no pole, but they'd devise a list of friends and teachers to receive May baskets (Miriam's mother let her write the list, even though it took much longer) and assemble cones of construction paper, filling them with chocolates at the bottom and bouquets of lilacs and pansies and bearded irises on top. They'd stack the baskets into a cardboard carton that they'd load in the station wagon. At each house, Miriam's mother would let the car idle while

Miriam scooted out to set a basket on a stoop, ring the doorbell, and run. They'd zoom away cackling as Miriam peered back to see if the recipient had spotted them.

The recipients were the same people who had called Miriam and emailed her and called again after her mother's death. Miriam kept saying no: no, there would be no funeral, no, she didn't need help sorting her mother's things, no, she didn't want to get coffee and talk about her feelings. The enormity of Miriam's loss was not going to be dulled by sharing it. Miriam would mourn in her own way, and if that didn't suit the rest of the world, the rest of the world could fuck the fuck off.

Only now did she consider, her blouse damp and wrinkled, her face and nose hot and puffy, that by keeping all the grief to herself, she'd also just plain kept to herself. Her roommate got through to her, sometimes, because she hadn't known Miriam's parents and didn't want to reminisce.

"People love to help," Miriam's mother had said after Miriam's dad had passed. "Miriam, let them."

Miriam hadn't believed her mother back then, but she also hadn't been an elementary school teacher, someone who mattered in a small town. Part of the fabric of the place, even if it was the extreme far frayed edge, shut in a car door, dragged for miles.

Now, as a community leader, Miriam decided she would take on a special project to bolster the town's morale. May Day would be her day. A May Pole would do for now, and further, would help the children learn their cultural heritage. The children were of German stock. And she had all that yarn, which would work just as well as ribbons to wrap the pole. She could honor her mother this way too. Her mother's long-delayed funeral ceremony. Miriam would bring a few balls of yarn a day to her classroom and store it in the supply closet so she'd be ready when the calendar flipped from April to May.

Maybe Miriam could make a real show, invite town dignitaries, if there were any. She supposed her landlord, Karl, qualified. They'd need to track down a big tree trunk or utility pole to serve as the May Pole. She could ask friends to come, too, if she made any in the next month.

That afternoon, Miriam told the students about the May Pole and showed them the book with the pictures of little German children all in white with flower crowns, circling the pole with ribbons. They listened. She described the yarn she would bring them. They liked the sound of all the colors. They asked if they could wrap the May Pole themselves. Miriam said sure, come May Day. Jericho asked if they could set the pole on fire. She told him the book hadn't said anything about that.

wWWw

After school that day Miriam did two things. First, she slit the spine of *Teaching Is Learning* and wadded up the loose pages, all 837 of them. With three months of teaching under her belt, she had reached a point in her journey where she knew more than the text. Example one: the new lessons she'd soon design all about family heritage and pagan (actually, better call them "folk") rituals.

Second, she sliced open the tape on the cardboard box that held her mother's and Fancy's ashes. The name of the crematory, listed on the return address, was Forget-Me-Not, damn it all.

Inside the cardboard box were two more knotty pine boxes, unlabeled, which seemed like a gross oversight on Forget-Me-Not's part. Miriam lifted each box and tried to judge who was who based on weight. Surely her mother would be heavier than Fancy. The boxes were beautiful, really—a warm honey hue, smooth and cool on her palm. Her mother had selected the style for her father's box to match her décor, and Miriam had simply ordered two more of the same boxes when the time came. She set all three on the mantel—her parents on either side, and the box she believed held Fancy in the middle. Looking at them didn't hurt. In fact, it gave her a little peace. But then she imagined Karl entering her home on some trumped-up excuse—changing air filters, checking the caulk on the windows—and pawing at her loved ones. She stowed them back in the cardboard carton her mother and Fancy had come in, along with the wadded *Teaching Is Learning* pages to keep the boxes from banging against each other. And under the bed they all went.

uuuuu

That weekend, Miriam dreamed she was eating a battery sandwich. AAAs on rye toast. Her teeth vibrated even after she awoke. It took her a few moments to realize that what disturbed her had been outdoor noises. Who was out at two in the morning and what the hell were they doing? Culvert was so silent at night that once a loud cricket had jolted Miriam awake.

She peered through the parted curtains. Lumbering down the street with funereal slowness was a line of Mack trucks with only their fog lights on. The low, chest-rattling rumble reminded Miriam of her old dorm in Boston, under which Red Line trains used to run.

Wide awake, Miriam pulled on her robe and boots and stepped outside. The cold air held the familiar faint scent of the pigs and another odor, stranger and more metallic, like how a hand smells after it touches a brass doorknob.

She could solve this mystery, at least. As the sixth and final truck growled by, Miriam stepped off the porch to follow the procession. The trucks rolled so slowly that she easily kept up, though she tried not to get so close the drivers might spy her in a mirror. She was grateful that her robe, like most of her wardrobe, was black. As the trucks passed by houses, townsfolk emerged and joined the parade on foot. Miriam fell back farther into the darkness. She easily could have called out to the shadowy figures close ahead of her, whom she likely would have known in daylight, but instinct held her back.

The engines roared, and metal clunked against metal in the truck beds. Everyone else wore bathrobes too. No one spoke. The procession tromped for a long time, past the edge of town, across the railroad tracks, and out into open countryside. At the lighted sign for Durftig Farms, everyone streamed down a dirt path through a field, raising a flock of crows. The rich smell of poop, urine, and blood made Miriam wish she could zip her nostrils shut.

The ground turned spongy. Thick mud weighed down Miriam's

boots. Still the group pushed forward, slower now, toward the back of the compound. The pigs woke at the ruckus, and Miriam could hear them in the cages, rattling the bars and stomping and huffing. A high urgent squeak from a far pen made Miriam's skin itch.

The trucks backed up to the three large open lakes of shit—hog lagoons—and the townsfolk hopped up on the bumpers to unlatch the tailgates. Nothing happened for maybe five minutes, but then the truck beds tipped back, and out rolled dozens of big metal barrels like crime-show murderers might use for their victims. The barrels landed with hollow, sloshing plops—some straight into the lagoons, some just outside. Miriam couldn't see clearly because the scene was lit only by the trucks' fog lights and brake lights, but it seemed as though the townsfolk pulled the barrels into the lagoons with big shepherds' crooks. The barrels floated briefly before the lagoons sucked them down, belching forth stench. The surface of the lagoons shone ruby red. While everyone's attention was turned to the sinking barrels, Miriam ventured closer. The words printed on the doors of the trucks read, "Scharf Industries."

A particularly fierce wave of reek sent Miriam stumbling against an upturned hog feeder, and two townsfolk turned at the sound.

"Hey," one of them called. "Come here."

Miriam ran across the farm lot, through the gate, and all the way home, pausing once to vomit against a neighbor's mailbox. Farm mud sloughed from her boots with each stride. She shucked off her boots at the door and took a frenzied shower, scrubbing her body much too hard with her loofah. She climbed back into bed, damp and vanilla scented, her heart still thumping in her chest.

In the morning she wondered whether she'd actually walked all the way to the lagoons and seen the townsfolk with the barrels, or if that might not have been part of her dream as well. Her boots still held a thin crust of fresh, smelly mud, but all of the soil in the town stunk, and it had rained off and on for the last three days. The mud could have come from anywhere. She couldn't think of any other wet patches she'd encountered, but her memory seemed to get worse by the day.

wMm

The next morning, a Saturday, thankfully, she had a little time to consider what she'd seen at the hog farm. Illegal dumping. But of what? Clearly, something the townsfolk never hoped to retrieve. And so many people had joined together toward that shared goal. No one had talked. Everyone moved in a coordinated fashion. The whole episode seemed well rehearsed, as though the townsfolk all knew what to do already. Miriam wondered if she could sneak back into the farm to take a sample of the soil around the lagoon. The gate had always been shut tight and wrapped with heavy chain when she'd passed it before.

Her doorbell rang. She'd known Karl would return, but she'd hoped it would take him longer. Her stomach hurt and she was in no mood to socialize. Her whole body felt weak. Plus, the other day she'd noticed that a few panties from her matching bra and panty sets had gone missing. She imagined Karl in his McMansion on the other side of town, football game on, recliner reclined, her prettiest thong draped over his nose, huffing deeply. She rolled off the couch, where she'd been reading her book about May Poles, and army crawled under the picture window to peer through the peephole. She wasn't going to let him in; she just wanted to see him. Well, maybe she would let him in. She was bored and lonely, which was not a good reason. But maybe she could get her panties back. The bras weren't nearly as cute on their own.

A woman about her mom's age stood on the stoop. She held a cardboard briefcase printed with stars. Little wire glasses slid down her nose, glasses like Miriam's mom's, and just like her mom, this woman tilted her head back to peer through the lenses with her large, kind eyes.

Miriam opened the door. "Hello there," the woman said. "Welcome to the neighborhood. May I come in?"

Miriam stepped back to let her pass. She had been so busy teaching the last few months that she hadn't been diligent about cleaning (though her roommate, and her parents for that matter, would attest that tidiness never was among her virtues). Cans of seltzer water lined her coffee table. Worksheets sprayed across the floor. A half-empty pot of black beans festered in the sink.

Miriam moved her wads of papers out of the way, and they sat together on the couch. The woman cleared a space on the coffee table and began to unload little cobalt glass vials from her suitcase. They were all labeled with names like Sun Echo and Desert Lore and Ethereal Coriander.

"This one's good for tension," the woman said, dotting a few drops of Above the Fray on her wrist and raising it for Miriam to smell. It was familiar somehow, like pesto.

"Is that basil?" Miriam asked.

"Very good! And sea buckthorn."

"Nice," Miriam said. She was ordinarily not the sort to get excited about woo-woo products, and the pamphlets the woman pushed on her had a professional look that made Miriam suspect the poor woman had fallen into a pyramid scheme. But there was no harm in listening.

"Have you been having any difficulties? Abdominal distress? Headaches? Irritability? Tingling in the feet and hands? Sense of looming helplessness and despair? I have oils for them all."

"What's the last oil smell like? The despair one?" Miriam asked. Those symptoms fit her to a T, now that the woman mentioned it.

"Oh, just peppermint. It's also good for cellulite," the woman said. She was eyeing Miriam's teaching supplies. "What grade?"

"Third. Though they aren't reading at anywhere near their grade level. Or reading at all, really. It's pretty bad."

"Have you worked with children much? How do they compare to other students you've had?" The woman slid her glasses down and moved closer to Miriam so she could really see her face. Miriam caught a whiff of lavender that reminded her so strongly of the lotion her mother had used after baths that she sniffed greedily at the air.

"I haven't been teaching long," Miriam said. "This is my first class."

"Bless your heart, your very first class," the woman said. "These students."

"You don't have a scent that makes you forget who you are, or what's happening, do you? That numbs it all down?"

"That's good you don't drink the tap water," the woman said, nodding at the seltzer cans. She sighed. "You aren't going to buy any oils, are you?"

"I'm sorry, but I don't think I am," Miriam said. "Maybe you'd want to stay for a while, though? I could make us some coffee right now."

"Oh, no," the woman said. "I couldn't possibly. If you ever stop teaching at the school, though, please do look me up. And if you notice any symptoms, keep the oils in mind. They aren't much, but I do believe they help a little. And don't do any gardening. Or drink the water." She handed Miriam a card. Miriam smelled the woman's lavender smell again. She remembered how when she was little, her mother would lay her on the counter by the kitchen sink and tip Miriam's head back into the bowl and shampoo her hair with those lavender-scented hands. Beauty shop, they'd called it. The warm water flowing, her mother's small strong hands under the nape of her neck.

The woman's business card had a picture of a tabby cat in a witch's hat riding a sparkling broom through the cosmos. It said, "Jenny Winkler, Independent Karma Oils Consultant."

Mrs. Winkler was opening the door to leave. "Mrs. Winkler!" Miriam called, running to stop her, "Mrs. Winkler! Did you used to teach third grade?"

Mrs. Winkler rushed down the stairs on Miriam's porch, still tilting her chin up to hold her glasses in place, and she tripped. Her suitcase popped open, scattering her oils. Miriam yelped, both for her new acquaintance and for the image that she couldn't shake, a woman falling down the stairs, face and palms first.

Miriam helped Mrs. Winkler up. She brushed off Mrs. Winkler's little suitcase and refilled it with the oils. Mrs. Winkler's palms were badly scraped.

"Look," Miriam said. "You're bleeding on your suitcase. Come back in. I'll just get the Neosporin." Miriam didn't have any Neosporin, but Mrs. Winkler had no way of knowing that, and if Miriam got her back inside, she'd ask Mrs. Winkler all sorts of questions about the students and the town. Finally, a chance for straight answers.

Mrs. Winkler paused as if considering Miriam's offer, but then a black pickup, notable for its age (brand new) and size (bigger than most) cruised by slowly, revving the engine. As the driver turned the corner, he deployed an air horn that trumpeted Woody Woodpecker's song, and he sped away. Without a word, Mrs. Winkler turned and scuffed down the road away from Miriam. Miriam watched Mrs. Winkler, expecting her to knock at the house next door, or the one after that, but she didn't stop at any others. Only Miriam's.

The bird's crazy laugh echoed in Miriam's head for a long time afterward. Mrs. Winkler's card had no contact information on it. Miriam turned the stiff paper over hoping for a handwritten note, but there was only a coupon for 15 percent off. No way to write, no way to call. Miriam could only hope the old teacher would come back to her.

wmm

Miriam was pitching in a class softball game, part of her effort to raise the children's energy level through exercise, when something awful happened. She had backpedaled to snag a fly ball and she stepped right into the hole the children had dug to bury beer cans. Her hands flew back to break her fall, and her full weight landed on her pinky. The pain radiated through her hand and shot up her elbow and shoulder. The children surrounded her as she sat panting on the dusty infield. They looked much taller from her low perspective. She plunged the hurt finger into her mouth to shield it from view. The pinky felt wrong. Dirt coated, it tasted metallic and strange, and her tongue numbed in a line along where it rested.

Miriam stood and seized the ball, her pinky sticking out sideways in a parody of a dainty teacup grasp. She didn't want to show the students that she could be hurt. They sensed the change in her energy, though, and they left the game to cluster at the schoolyard fence. The wind whipped across the schoolyard, carrying the earthy, ammoniac funk of the hog farm. Miriam encouraged her students to jump up and down and take deep breaths. "You'll have more energy, I promise," she told them. "It's counterintuitive but true." She took a deep breath herself and retched at the smell. Ripe enough to gag a maggot, her mother would have said. "Whew, fresh air," Miriam gasped as she jogged in place in her pointy-toed loafers.

Later that day, her burning, broken finger stabilized with a piece of Scotch tape, she roamed the classroom while the students drew pictures to decorate a bulletin board. She admired a purple tree and many, many dinosaurs. One dinosaur seemed to have fur.

"What's his name?" Miriam asked the artist.

"Fancy," he said.

"Fancy that," Miriam said. "I knew a cat named Fancy."

"He's dead," the student said, pointing at his art. Miriam's heart beat rapidly.

"How did he die?" Miriam asked.

The student sat with his feet on his chair, his knees sticking up. "Squashed," he said, flapping his knees. Miriam didn't ask any more questions. The real Fancy would never have such a stupid look on his face—that open-mouthed gape scrawled in crayon. Fancy kept his mouth closed unless he was yowling or eating.

Next, Miriam inspected Kimmy Schneider's drawing of a naked man splayed across a desk, papers cascaded merrily to the ground. Despite the image's shaky lines, Miriam recognized a paperweight she'd given her father for his birthday, a rock painted to resemble a turtle. Kimmy pulled on Miriam's arm, pointing. "That there's a rhino, Miss Green, with some birds flapping around. Do you like it?" Kimmy asked. Her light blue eyes seemed guileless as a stand of blooming chicory along the roadside. Miriam nodded and hung Kimmy's drawing with the others.

wwww

Miriam got Mr. Kalt to cover her class one afternoon because she had a doctor's appointment in Dodge City. She needed a refill on her birth control pills—pointless on one hand because the chance of her having sex was somewhere between nil and less than nil, if such a thing were possible. But on the other hand, she skipped the off weeks so she hadn't had a period in three years and preferred to keep it that way.

Also, doing her job while on her monthly, as her mother had called it, didn't strike her as wise. She didn't want the students to see her moody and vulnerable.

She had considered driving to Salina to see her childhood doctor, but her mother and that doctor had been thick as thieves. Her mother was a minor hypochondriac, which she'd passed down to Miriam in the form of germaphobia. The doctor and her mother loved to go back and forth about her mother's self-diagnoses, the latest of which, MS, the doctor insisted was nothing more than grief at losing her husband, curable with time and sleep and maybe some Lexapro. Miriam could picture her old doctor's caring, searching eyes. She picked the first name on a list of Dodge City doctors.

Dr. Abel's office used to be a ranch house. The waiting room was the living room, and they'd even left the furnishings in place—heavy, artless oak curio cabinets and consoles, cobwebbed dried flowers on the coffee table, a duck decoy, a pink-and-blue print of an English country cottage surrounded by a garden that might, years earlier, have been the source of the sad ghostly posies on the coffee table today. The magazines were *Reader's Digest* and *TV Guide*. All that was missing was *Guideposts*.

The doctor himself looked like an older version of Mr. Kalt, heavier, with lighter hair and thick aviator-style glasses tinted yellow. Miriam checked for battery acid scars, but his hands were smooth, and a knot in the small of her back released.

He wrote up the prescription for the pills without a pelvic exam, which was a blessing. But then he asked if she had any other concerns.

"Dr. Abel," she said, her voice even and low, "I'm concerned about my third-grade students, and the town where I live. Everyone in it. I think there might be something wrong."

Dr. Abel chewed his lip and stabbed the button of his clicking pen into his knee a few times.

"Wrong how?" he asked.

"Well, they are slow on the uptake. I speak to them and it seems as if they can't understand. They are quick to anger. They're either really drowsy or hyper. It's just not right," Miriam finished. She had only given him the barest glimmering of the problem, but much of it lay in her gut. The wrongness exceeded language.

"You said you've never taught before? How's your support system?" he said.

"Oh, it's fine. The principal is good to me. And there's Janet in Boston, who runs the program, though I don't talk to her much. Elizabeth, my old roommate. And, well, I guess that's about it."

"No friends in town? What about family?"

"My parents both died last year. There's no one else."

"Good lord. You're still grieving. Maybe you'd like some antidepressants?"

"I was thinking you could help me figure out if the hog farm on the edge of town is making everyone sick," Miriam said.

"You're thinking what? Trichinosis?"

"I don't know what that is."

"It's nasty," he said.

"In *Jane Eyre*," Miriam said, "Jane's little friend dies because their school is low-lying and an unhealthy miasma gathers around it. I suspect bad air. And I came across a whole group of townsfolk one night moving barrels from the battery factory to the hog lagoons. What was in them?"

"You seem like a smart individual. Do you have a tendency to create problems when none exist so you have some drama in your life? Many women do."

"Did you know that the Rod of Asclepius actually represents a May Pole?"

"What's the Rod of Asclepius?"

"A snake twirled around a pipe. The symbol of your profession. I'll bet you thought it was the caduceus. But you're wrong. The caduceus has two snakes and wings on top. It's the staff of Hermes, the symbol of commerce."

Miriam stood over the old doctor now, and his eyes were hidden by the glare of the fluorescents off his glasses. His hands were raised in supplication.

"What you should have asked me," Miriam said, "is 'what's a May

Pole?'" She would have been happy to tell him that whatever attached to the May Pole gained access to arcane knowledge due to the May Pole's position between earth and the heavens. She wouldn't mind having a conversation with that twined snake. She could stand to learn a thing or two, though she was the teacher.

On her way out, Miriam stole the head off the duck decoy. She couldn't begin to imagine why.

ⁿⁿⁿⁿⁿ

One day in early April, some students in the back of the classroom invented a new game called "electric chicken." Miriam thought it was sweet how they'd all joined hands, until she got closer and saw that their hair was standing on end. She asked them to describe the rules. They explained that they'd jammed a frayed power cord in an outlet, and the current flowed from the outlet through their hands, shocking them, until one student couldn't take it and had to let go.

"Does it hurt?" Miriam asked.

"Oh yeah," Cy said. "It gets worse each time somebody drops out."

"That's because the same amount of current is flowing across less area," Miriam explained. "The voltage, or perhaps it's the amperes, is increased. What does the winner get?"

"Chicken dinner."

"Not pork?" Miriam asked. "Durftig Farms?"

Cy smiled. He'd just lost his front teeth by running into a bar on the playground. His prominent incisors and red gums reminded Miriam of a wolf's mouth, somehow, and further reinforced the notion that we are animals, kin to animals, even when our handbags match our nail polish.

ⁿⁿⁿⁿⁿ

Later that week, she told Mr. Kalt about Kimmy's art. He said, "Yeah, those Schneiders, they've never been right. Kimmy has an uncle whose eyelids got put on backward."

"By whom?" Miriam asked.

"By God," Mr. Kalt said straight-faced. Then he busted up. Something about Mr. Kalt's guffaw reminded her vaguely of her landlord. That was unsurprising due to the concentrated population here. Karl was probably his cousin. "No, I'm kidding. Some two-bit doctor out in Dodge. His pet donkey bit them off, and they wrestled them out of the ass's mouth and got them on ice, but the doc got flustered when confronted with uncovered peepers. He reattached them all right, just wrong way out."

Names had mattered in Boston, but in a different way, as an arbiter of class rather than an identifier of traits. The Brahmins. Good old New England families with pinched English names who'd possessed money and desirable real estate for centuries. In the midsize town where she'd grown up, there was no accumulation of generations. Even the Native Americans, before the white settlers hemmed them into reservations, had been wanderers. The Kansa translated as "People of the Wind." Now in the eastern part of the state, and even the middle, from where Miriam hailed, people flushed up and down the Mississippi too fast to grow roots. They swarmed in from the little towns along the smaller tributaries—the Smoky Hill, the Platte, the Solomon, White Dog and Red Willow Creeks—and zoomed out by airplane to the coasts, as Miriam had done.

Drifting back west was her big mistake.

Mr. Kalt said, "I heard you saw a doctor out Dodge City way. Dr. Weber's always been good enough for us in these parts."

"I wanted to see a female doctor," Miriam said. The lie was out before she knew it.

"Oh yes," Mr. Kalt said. "That makes sense." He sat back in his big padded chair and nodded a few times as though he were convincing himself.

"Mr. Kalt," Miriam asked, "do you know why a bunch of trucks from the battery factory would drop barrels into the hog lagoons?"

Kalt jumped as if she'd pricked him. He peered at her, blinking. "The hog lagoons? Are you sure? What were you doing out there?"

"I don't know," Miriam said. "I might have been dreaming. But my boots had mud on them, and my stomach hasn't felt right since. I can barely keep anything down.

"Well water," Mr. Kalt said. "That's why. It takes some getting used to. Bunch of dissolved minerals. Bottle it and give it a toney French name, and you're sitting on a jackpot. Like that artisan salt company down the road with their fancy green stuff. It's all just salt."

The light through Kalt's window had taken on a golden hue. The sun grew brighter, and each day now lasted a bit longer, Miriam's favorite time of the year. May Day would arrive before she knew it.

wwwm

A couple Jehovah's Witnesses from Wichita, young men in clip-on ties and short-sleeve dress shirts, knocked at Miriam's door one Saturday, and after she ascertained they weren't Karl, she eagerly invited the young men in.

"Excuse the mess," she told them as she cleared piles of papers and plates with stuck on shredded cheese from the couch so they could sit down. "It's just so rare I get visitors," she said, smiling broadly as she handed them mugs of tea. "How's Wichita? Last time I was there, I went to the Banana Republic."

"It's good," the taller one said. He rubbed his hands on the legs of his pants. "Would you mind if I shared a bit of scripture with you? Then you could say how you feel about it."

"Is the Banana Republic still there? They had the best sales," Miriam said. If she could just keep them from the metaphysical subject, they could all have a nice visit.

"As you can see," the shorter one with the faint mustache said, "we have this tract we're sharing with our neighbors. The passage we'll read helps to shed some light on two questions: what happens to us when we die, and is there any hope for the dead?" As he said the last five words, he tapped on the tract's glossy cover, and it felt to Miriam like his thumb had jabbed her pineal gland, loosing a rush of euphoria, or perhaps dysphoria. Hope! The dead were dead, beyond hope, and best beyond our ruminations too.

Miriam stood and waited for the young men to rise. "I totally forgot I'm a Jehovah's Witness already, so you don't need to convert me. Isn't that great? One more saved."

The Jehovah's Witnesses' talk of the afterlife had yanked her gaze straight back to her grief. She didn't like it. Miriam hardly thought about her parents anymore. The grief used to be a black spot right in the center of her visual field, so she only caught the rest of life in the corners. But now that she had these new problems, the mystery of her students' behavior, and of their parents' midnight trip to the pig farm, the black spot was banished to the extreme lower edge of her view. She might not see it for a week, not at all, as long as she kept her head held high and remembered never to look down.

She found a tract under her mat the next day, with a note that said, "You need the word more than I do."

wmm

Whenever Miriam walked around town, the residents looked at her like she was an alien visitor. Were you part of the midnight procession? Miriam longed to ask each person she passed, but she was scared to let anyone know what she'd seen that night. She regretted telling Principal Kalt.

Wherever she turned, the wind rasped the plains and blew soil in her face. The big pickups driven by her students' parents zoomed past when she jogged on the road shoulder and honked as though her presence offended them. After she nearly got beaned on the back of the head by a particularly protuberant wing mirror, she quit jogging.

Her body, anyway, needed rest. After a day of teaching, it was all she could do to shuck off her pencil skirt. She felt like a husk scraped clean. The ringing blare of the students' high voices had started to trigger a vestigial impulse to flatten her ears. That was impossible, of course, so she'd grit her teeth instead. Her feet burned, her jaw ached, and her mouth constantly tasted metal. She related a little to the burned guy in the post office. Old before her time. After story time, she caught herself gasping a few times before she heaved herself up off the ground. "You

young people will be the death of me," she'd tell her students. They
blinked up with their eyes the pale blue of skim milk. "That was a joke,"
she said. "You can tell a joke is no good if you have to explain it."

She drove out to cell phone range a couple times, listened to the
messages from her old roommate, Elizabeth, and buzzed straight back
to Culvert. Her roommate's voicemails begged her to pick up and say
how she was doing, if the kids were rowdy or tame, if the buildings
in town were ramshackle or quaint, if she was dating a cute cowboy
yet. The only ranching happening near Culvert was pigs, and the workers in the processing facility wore tall black rubber boots and leather
aprons. A leather apron was almost like chaps.

uurun

Miriam closely monitored her students' skin, which was, if anything,
bluer. She had a piece of blue construction paper that she'd surrepti-
tiously raise to their arms as a baseline. Also, the students' behavior
was fishy. They didn't get joy from the right places. They spent a whole
recess standing around a dead robin, taking turns poking it with a
stick. She felt a little like her mother, eager to diagnose. Paging Dr. Miriam. Something had to be done.

Miriam visited the post office one Saturday morning in mid-April.
The same very pale clerk with the acid burns manned the counter. He
had been growing out his hair and now he wore the sides of his mane
pinned up at the top of his head with Miriam's tortoiseshell barrette.
He was reading a pamphlet called "New Postal Rates and You: Don't
Get Caught Short," which he didn't put down when the bell tinkled,
heralding Miriam's arrival. She waited a little while and said, "Excuse
me."

The clerk jerked up and glared at her.

"Riveting reading?" Miriam asked.

"Someone has to keep up standards," he said. "The mail doesn't mail
itself, you know."

"You do a fine job," Miriam said.

The clerk sniffed delicately and ran his scarred hand over the spine of his pamphlet as though he longed to continue reading.

"I'll bet you know where everyone lives," Miriam said. She had spent the morning googling Mrs. Winkler's address, but she'd come up dry.

"That's confidential," he snapped.

"The woman I'm looking for, Mrs. Winkler, stopped by my home. She was going to sell me some essential oils, but I didn't have my wallet. You'd be helping her if you could just direct me to her home, or even let me know where she hangs out." Miriam smiled and nodded to encourage him. She wanted to ask Mrs. Winkler about the students' hyperactivity and lethargy, their blue skin, but first she needed to find her.

"Mrs. Blinkler?" he asked, cupping his palm to his ear.

"Blinkler?" Miriam said. "Winkler! She taught third grade here for decades. She was probably even your teacher."

"I don't know any Blinklers," he said, "and I'd remember. That's a very unusual name."

As she turned to leave, he said, "You want some stamps?"

wmm

When Miriam returned to her house after the trip to the post office, there was a note from her landlord, Karl, wedged in the mailbox. In dark all caps, he'd scrawled: "SUMP PUMP BUSTED. DOWN IN BASEMENT." The sump pump had been sputtering sadly for a few weeks now, though it hadn't rained. The machine seemed to have its own agenda, and although she knew she should have called her landlord to keep him abreast, she couldn't bear to waste time in awkward conversation while he ogled her breasts. The key to being a true gentleman, she'd have to tell him eventually, was keeping your head angled toward the female interlocutor's face, so if your eyes drifted downward you maintained plausible deniability.

She thought about bringing Karl a glass of water. It was no doubt dusty and disgusting in the basement, stuffed with spiders and many-legged insects that she'd occasionally seen emerge, pale and slow-moving, to expire on the carpet. She wondered if he'd drink the water she offered without knowing where it had come from. She popped open a bottle of water for herself instead and turned up the air-conditioning so she couldn't hear him thrashing below her. How had he figured out the trouble with the sump pump? Snooping. A pervy agenda Miriam preferred not to explore. And why did he insist on fixing the sump pump himself? If he were as wealthy as he pretended, why was he the one inhaling cobwebs? Either he wasn't that rich, or he wanted to get close to her, even if it was through a subfloor. She hoped he was broke.

She swept the dirtiest dishes from her coffee table to her sink and sat on the couch with her hands poised on her laptop keyboard. She googled "child lethargy stomachache." Sites popped up that suggested poor diet and lack of exercise. As she read, she pulled at a hangnail. She put her pinky finger in her mouth and ripped the loose sliver of skin. The flesh on her finger stung so she sucked it. Since her softball accident, the pinky had healed as thick as her ring finger and slightly crooked. Still, it had been worth it. Exercise was good for the students. Softball had been a decent start, despite her injury. Maybe next week she could bring the students fruit from Dodge City.

But she remembered how her body felt when she was a child: good. The buoyant flight of her mind and her limbs, despite her love for peanut butter and jelly sandwiches and Planters brand cheese balls. Diet alone couldn't explain this sad crew.

She added "blue skin" to her search and the results got much more specific. Pages upon pages appeared, from the EPA, the CDC, HHS. Her heart batted against her ribs. She read about parts per million and industrial exposures and abatement and IQ loss and poor bone growth and muscle tone. Hyperactivity. Poor hearing. Learning problems. She decided to order an at-home lead test and, to get free shipping, a book of one thousand reward stickers she could affix to the students' worksheets. She'd give herself the test, and then, in three to four weeks, she'd know. Before the end of the semester, even, she might understand how to help the students.

Just as she submitted her order, the basement door creaked open and a silver man-sized blob waddled in, crinkling like aluminum foil with each step.

"Why are you wearing that suit?" Miriam asked her landlord. Karl was wrapped like a Christmas ham. He removed the breathing apparatus and goggles and took a few huge gasping breaths, which made him cough. With each spasm, dust settled on the linoleum and the carpet beyond.

"Mind if I use your shower?" he asked. "That's funny, isn't it? That's how pornos start." His face looked like a raccoon's in reverse—the eyes and muzzle pale and the rest of the face, exposed, nearly black.

"I do mind, actually," Miriam said. "I was just going to take a bath."

"That's the next line in the script!" Karl crowed. "Now I say, 'Let me help you get out of those tight pants.'" They both looked at Miriam's legs, which were covered in plaid flannel culottes that ended below the knee. Her pale, hairy calves peeked from the hem.

"Why are you wearing that suit?" Miriam repeated.

"Oh, safety," Karl said. "You never can tell what's in the dust."

"Like what?" Miriam said. Karl moved toward the couch and hovered over Miriam's shoulder, peering at the computer screen.

"Lead?" he said. "What's that all about?"

"You tell me," Miriam said.

Karl slapped his silver crinkling thigh and gave voice to a mighty chuckle. "You're something else," he told her. His face didn't match his laugh. He looked pensive.

"Besides," Miriam said, "it's not lead, it's lead like leadership. A test for leaders. Like *What Color Is Your Parachute?* You heard of that?"

"You show me your parachute and I'll show you mine," Karl said. His rich, stagey laugh followed him out the door and down to his enormous black truck. Miriam locked the door behind him. She poured herself some water from the tap but decided it might be better to have a canned seltzer instead.

wmm

The lead test never arrived. To check on her package, she drove to the post office behind another Mack truck hauling steel barrels, all of which were stenciled with the words "Hazardous Waste." The barrels leaked a reddish-brown slurry. When she turned into the lot, the truck continued on, toward Durftig Farms.

The same pale young man worked the counter. This time he wore Miriam's black fleece headband with the hole for her ponytail. He'd turned the hole to the front and drawn a shock of his white-blond hair through it, an odd fountain.

Miriam tried to remember why she'd driven to the post office. More and more now, she'd arrive somewhere and wrack her brain to determine a cause. She'd heard of absentminded professors, but surely a third-grade teacher could keep her wits. "I ordered something. It didn't show up," Miriam finally told him. "Online it says it's out for delivery. But it was never delivered."

"You got a tracking number?" the young man said. He played a farming game on his phone in which he grew pigs in the ground, as if they were wheat. There was even a little scythe to harvest them once they were full size. He ran the scythe under the pigs' hooves and they popped free, lying on their sides until the farmer collected them in his bushel basket. The pigs never stopped smiling.

Miriam fumbled for her phone. She showed him the order confirmation email with the tracking number.

"You looking to get the lead out?" he said.

"Nope, just want to see if there's any here."

"Lead? What makes you think there's lead of all things?"

"Well," Miriam said, "battery factories produce lead as a byproduct. If it isn't disposed of properly, it can leak into the soil and make its way to the water supply. You didn't see anything weird when you worked at Scharf did you?"

"Hmm," he said. "I don't know about all of that. I do know it's hard to get all the packages delivered. Especially because you order so much. I guess this one just didn't work out."

"That's it?" Miriam asked.

"Sure," he said. "Unless you want to buy some stamps?"

Miriam noticed that the clerk had picked up the post-office tele-phone as she left. He was watching her with the receiver to his ear.

wmm

Miriam drove east until she got a signal and called an EPA hotline to report a potential environmental violation, but the line rang and rang. The new president, elected after her father's death but before her mother's, belonged to the same political party as the governor of Kansas, who'd chopped the public education budget. The president had slashed the EPA's funding badly, and now it seemed no one remained to answer the phone. Rural and Rising got some federal money in the form of grant programs due to be cut, and Janet had been sending increasingly panicky emails to her enormous contact list begging that everyone call their congressperson to stand up for the young poor of the countryside. Miriam hadn't yet made her plea to her new congressman. He was a tall man with a wide bland face, watery eyes, invisible brows, a pouf of gray hair, and a startled smile, who fought fiercely against immigration and corporate taxes and healthcare access. He most likely had truly deranged sexual proclivities involving produce, schoolchildren, or trips to Thailand, maybe all three together, somehow.

She tried Elizabeth, who answered out of breath on the second ring. Her old roommate had gotten a great deal on one of those at-home exercise bikes with the TV screens where a fit person coaches you through workouts. "I'm addicted!" Elizabeth declared. "Which is a good thing because right downstairs from my apartment is a French bakery. It smells like heaven! The macarons there aren't quite as good as a place out in Georgetown. The little shells are a touch too thick and not crisp enough at the edges. The bakery is better than drinking though. I've decided to take a week off. I could practically hear my liver screaming. Don't you wonder what's happening inside your body?"

"The only thing people out here are addicted to is meth," Miriam said, which wasn't accurate (it was fentanyl) but would please Elizabeth because it reinforced a story Elizabeth thought she knew.

"Ha!" Elizabeth said. "But how are you doing, really? You never call."

"I told you there's no reception. Hey, you don't know anybody who works for the EPA, environmental justice, anything like that?"

"Hmm . . . I can ask around. Oops! The lady's back. Time to pedal. Call me soon!"

Macarons! Miriam couldn't even imagine.

Miriam stopped at the grocery store in Dodge City and bought ten cases of bottled water. She would use it to drink, cook, and brush her teeth. She also got a package of those strawberry, chocolate, and vanilla wafer cookies, western Kansas's closest approximation to the macaron. When she was little, she'd eat the wafers first and compact the cream filling into a big sticky ball and eat that last. A redneck truffle. Though her family hadn't been rednecks, and that was an offensive term, anyway. She called herself a redneck a lot in Boston. Why did she like to play into those easy stereotypes so much? Part of her found them funny; another part got hurt by them; and a third part, perhaps the dominant one, liked to feel hurt.

After Miriam returned and unloaded her supplies, she discovered a website with an anonymous form to report polluters, but she didn't want to leave any contact information, and her answers to the prompts would look vague at best, like the rantings of a nut at worst. "Describe the nature of the violation, including violator, violation method, and affected subjects: Well, I'm not sure if a violation did in fact occur. But the students are only getting worse. Every day, they struggle to lift their heads from the desks and mutter strange half-sentences. I'm a teacher, I should mention. I suspect lead. From the battery factory probably. Scharf. I saw a midnight dumping at the hog lagoon. So many silver barrels. I don't always feel right myself. My warmer-hued lipsticks no longer match my complexion. Instead of Cinnamon and Fawn Sunrise, which had always been my go-tos, now I gravitate to Wild Rose and Saucy, which is a cool mauve, medium in intensity. Lead turns your skin blue. The internet told me that. Could you please come check the soil? And the water. We are all affected."

After she hit "submit," the relief didn't quite come, so she dashed off a note to the watery-eyed congressman and read the regional news. There was a story about a bunch of men trapped in a salt mine a few hundred miles to her east. She wondered if their confinement brought them any comfort. It circumscribed the range of available life choices. She read another news story about the fifteenth anniversary of the death of a woman from Miriam's hometown who'd drowned in a water feature in her own landscaping, right in her front yard. Miriam thought she knew a little bit how that woman must have felt: You try to beautify something, leave it better, and what happens? Despite your own good intentions, you wind up in a mess. The woman left behind two young sons. The thought of those two motherless boys stung Miriam's eyes. There was no mention of the father.

uMMm

It was a week before May Day. The sky had darkened and yellowed. Miriam described to her students how on May 1 in Malta, the rich hid an assortment of pickled and potted meats and other delicacies, including live pigs and chickens, for the poor to search out, and the finder was the keeper. "Can you imagine," Miriam asked, eyes wide, "how it might feel to stumble across a great big glistening sausage in the woods?" She sketched a simple floor plan of the Maltese Grandmaster's Palace on the chalkboard and urged the students to come to the board to draw in the hidden trays of deviled eggs. "Where would you stash the ham, had you been a Maltese noble, Kimmy?" Miriam said. The wind rose shrilly, like a child wailing as loudly as it possibly could. It rushed damp air through the open windows. The barometric pressure dropped. A few students glanced outside or pinned their papers to their desks with their fists, but most watched Miriam's presentation, rapt. The class rarely spoke of anything but the May Pole now, and they all seemed to respond with considerably more attention than her earlier lessons, though Jericho Jungnickel never did grasp that there wasn't some big finish, such as setting the Pole alight, or his new idée fixe, bashing the Pole like a piñata. "No bashing, no flames, just rebirth," was Miriam's refrain. Miriam taught for real now, to hell with the lesson plans or year-end learning assessments. She couldn't sleep nights for the ideas spiraling through her, and not just her brain. Inspiration saturated her body. She pulled ideas from her fingertips, her kneecaps, her left butt cheek. Ideas! Good ideas flowing thick as the runoff from hog lagoons.

Kimmy Schneider had drawn a yellow chalk ham in the Maltese Grandmaster's bedroom closet. She seemed to waffle between hiding the deviled eggs in the scullery or the princess's bedchamber, but before she could sketch them in, a siren sounded—deeper than a police siren and much more drawn out. It crescendoed to a shrill high piercing note. The students fled for the hallway.

"Wait," Miriam said. "Hold on!" The sky in the window had greened to the hue of a healing bruise. She grabbed her purse from the supply closet and rushed after the children.

In the hallway she found all her students, all the teachers, all the other students, and Mr. Kalt sitting in a weird Child's Pose, facing the walls with their arms covering the backs of their heads and necks. Miriam dropped beside Mr. Kalt.

"I remember these," she said. "Tornado watches. We had them in Salina, too, though not too often." The wind and the siren tried to outdo each other with their moaning.

"Not a watch but a warning," Mr. Kalt said. "A watch is just if the conditions are right. A warning means a tornado was sighted on the ground. The siren signals the warning."

"Oh wow," Miriam said. "Are you scared?"

Mr. Kalt peeked through his armpit at her. "Nah. If these kids weren't here, I'd be back on the loading dock trying to get a good look."

"It's weird that this whole town might not exist tomorrow," Miriam said.

"Plenty have threatened this place. Nobody's got the better of us yet," Mr. Kalt said.

The children devised a game where one student would stand up, run along the line of bent bodies, and kick a classmate in the butt. The classmate would stand, the kid would slide into the vacant place in the line, and the game would continue, like an apocalyptic duck duck goose.

"Should I stop them?" Miriam asked Mr. Kalt.

"Nah," he said. "They're having fun. If a tornado does sweep in, how much safer do you really think the kids on ground would be?"

Right as the all-clear signal came, the same tone as the school dismissal bell, a small foot plonked Miriam's rump. She stood to confront the offender, but the student had already melted into the group of milling bodies. Mrs. Sheldrake winked at her as though they shared a joke. Perhaps Miriam herself was the joke. Surely a teacher wouldn't kick a colleague.

∼∽∼

After the tornado warning, Miriam assigned the students a final art project. She'd mixed clay out of salt and flour for heart sculptures that the students could decorate with flaky tempura paint. They'd present the baked clay hearts to loved ones at the May Pole event. It would be sweet. Miriam had spoken to Karl about the May Pole, and he offered to donate an old railroad tie she could stand upright, but she'd decided that the tetherball pole would work better.

Two students vomited after eating the clay. One boy had a bright ring of tempura paint all around his mouth. "I think it's egg based," Miriam said. "You aren't allergic to eggs, are you?" His face had started to redden and swell and he couldn't stop raking his fingernails over his cheeks and puffy eyelids. One more for the nurse's office. After Miriam put Tuxton in charge of the rest of the class, she marched the student down the hall.

When she returned, she found Jericho had chosen a more literal rendering for his heart, complete with aorta and valves.

Miriam paused over him. She liked it better when the students sat down because they looked smaller. "Very realistic. How did you know what a heart looks like?"

"I've seen a cow's," he said. "Heart attack!" he yelled, stabbing at

135

Kimmy with his art. Kimmy swooned dramatically, clasping the heart to her chest and collapsing across her desk in a fan of worksheets. Miriam gasped.

When she could speak, she said, "I think that's good enough for now. Let's leave these by the window to dry."

"Why do you have so much yarn in your house, Miss Green?" Cy asked as the students set their sticky hearts in the sun.

"How do you know I have so much yarn in my house?" Miriam asked.

Cy shrugged. He set down his heart and plucked up his rattail and stroked it. His mouth fell open in pleasure.

Miriam was already walking away when he said something. She was sure she'd heard wrong.

"What?" she said, turning to face him.

"You must miss your mom," he repeated.

"What?" she said again, more quietly.

"You don't live with her," Cy whispered. "I'd miss my mom."

𝓌𝓂𝓂𝓋

One day after school, Miriam discovered that Karl had entered her house without calling or leaving a note, as tenancy law dictated. She'd first noticed the characteristic piney odor of his cologne, the same smell Mr. Kalt had. It must have been the only cologne the town convenience store sold. Possibly it was Pine-Sol. Her laptop also lay open on the coffee table, and when she checked the browsing history, she found Karl had been shopping for windshield wipers and novelty beer steins. She surveyed the beer stein listings for a long time, marveling at the sheer variety: eagles flying airplanes, fish breaching the surface of lakes, sailors puffing pipes, and police dogs wearing sergeant's caps and aviator shades, all in brightly painted ceramic.

Her own browsing history tab was open, too, showing results from the last week when she'd researched lead contamination, but that didn't strike her as notable. Karl probably just hoped to see what sort of porn she liked. The sump pump no longer gurgled, which was a blessing.

wmm

Karl Scharf did something awfully nice the weekend before May Day. Miriam had sent an invitation to him and the other town VIPs: the sheriff, the high school football coach, the warden of the supermax just down the road in Goodland, and Karl's good buddy Vern, the elderly game warden, who wore his uniform and carried his gun even when off duty. Miriam had assumed her invitation to Karl would go unheeded, but then she'd heard an awful screeching from the direction of the school. She headed over, afraid some youths were torturing a cat, and she discovered Karl, shirtless and perspiring thickly in the sun. His circular saw shrilled. He spotted her and waved her over. He was assembling simple wooden risers facing the tetherball pole.

"You really think people will come?" Miriam asked, her hand at her brow and her eyes squinting against the day.

"Oh, sure," Karl said. "People are real curious about you, is the thing." He kept rubbing the head of his hammer on his palm, as if to remove a stubborn bit of stickum.

"This is very sweet," Miriam said. Her mother used to say that curiosity is the opening fanfare of friendship, or maybe that was *Teaching Is Learning*. Miriam's past and present had fused. When she tried to separate time, to draw out a single strand from the plied yarn of memory, the whole skein snarled until she longed to throw it all away and start over. A fresh hank, a new life, unblemished by the tangle of before.

"Come try it out," Karl urged, lightly patting the risers with the hammer.

Miriam shook her head.

"Come on, come on. Try it. Or maybe you'd prefer if the stands collapsed on a whole mess of third graders?"

"I'm not sure those are the only two options," Miriam said. She climbed the first tier anyway. There were no railings, and her weight rocked the structure. She stepped up to the next level, and the level after it. She imagined the tetherball pole all hung with yarns of different colors and the little boys and girls, her very own, who'd grasp the yarns and dance around the pole until they wrapped it so bright and pretty. They'd be dressed in short pants and in hats with ribbons on the brim, singing a song she'd taught them, "She'll Be Comin' Round the Mountain." Only after they'd learned the song did Miriam, intrigued by the sweet lyrics about lovers reuniting, learn the song was about the Rapture.

The risers shuddered. Miriam fell to her knees and clasped at the shifting boards, sure she'd topple. A splinter slid into her palm, sending a bright shaft of pain up the inside of her arm.

Karl hooted and jiggled the risers again, softer this time.

"What the heck, Mr. Kalt!" Miriam shouted.

"Say what? Mr. Kalt! Who's he? That principal? I'm Karl, your landlord!"

"Oh wow, sorry," Miriam said. "You remind me of Mr. Kalt."

"It won't wobble like that once I get the cross braces in. Shouldn't, anyway." He raised a gentlemanly hand to guide Miriam down, but sucking at her injured palm, she ignored his gesture.

"Hey," Karl said. "I was going to surprise you, but what the heck. My brother Eddie's a trusted advisor of Governor Rodriguez. Way high up. He thinks he might be able to get the governor here for your event. His wife, at least."

"Seriously?" Miriam said. "That's really nice, Karl."

"Well, it's not a sure thing," Karl said. He dropped a wrench on his toe and yelped.

"Don't you have people who could build this for you?" Miriam asked.

"Of course," Karl said, grinning, as he bent to pick up the wrench. "But this is a passion project." Miriam left him there, hammering and measuring and bellowing out a tune about a bullfrog.

Back on her couch, she worked the splinter out of her palm. She watched as blood filled the creases like tributaries on the map of an undiscovered country.

wwm

On May Day morning, the wind shifted from the direction of the hog lagoons to that of the battery factory, the fresh gale a good omen. The students roiled and teemed in their seats, and many of them had managed to arrive wearing the homemade lederhosen Miriam had suggested in a simply worded note to their parents: "White shirt, brown or green shorts, and suspenders. High white socks. If possible, a hat with a feather. You are invited to join Miss Green's third grade class for the May Pole during lunch (12:00 to 12:30). May Day (May 1) is a traditional way to celebrate the coming of spring. It is part of your HERITAGE."

Kimmy Schneider's feather, a long yellow tuft she might have plucked from Big Bird's wing, didn't stay long in her mesh-back baseball cap. She waved the feather like a baton, and when another student tried to grab it away, she stabbed the point of the feather right into the back of the student's hand, where it lodged like an arrow in a bull's-eye. The other student fell squalling, of course—Miriam would have as well. He tucked the injured hand against his chest, so he bled all down his white shirt. As Miriam hustled the student out toward the nurse's office, she could hear Kimmy shouting the words to "Yankee Doodle Dandy" and whooping while pounding her mouth with her palm like a Native American in a Western, patently offensive. "Cultural appropriation and gross stereotyping," Miriam muttered. A thought occurred to her: Were the lederhosen problematic, too? Nope, the little outfits were different because that's their own culture.

When Miriam returned to the classroom sans stabbing victim, the supply closet doors were flung open and the students had hurled all of the yarn out onto the floor of the classroom. She ordered them to put it back, but then she heard Jericho gagging by her desk. He'd been swallowing a long strand of superwash merino until the attached skein met his lips. She grabbed his body around the middle and tried to force the yarn back up using the Heimlich maneuver. But she couldn't get her arms around him to perform the procedure correctly. Miriam's mandatory CPR training had not covered this. She flipped Jericho faceup.

He'd stopped coughing. A length of yarn dangled damply over his chin. She grasped the end of the strand and pulled gently but firmly. The fiber was snarled and covered in spittle. At last she reached the end and Jericho gasped. Color flooded his face. His eyes crossed and uncrossed. He smiled. Miriam smiled back, glad to have helped in some small way.

She turned to reassure the class, but they weren't in their assigned seats. Nor in the entire classroom. Or the hallway. And she couldn't see them through the window out in the schoolyard, either. The swings swayed back and forth as though recently abandoned, but Miriam knew it was just the wailing wind. When she turned back to Jericho to ask if he knew the whereabouts of his classmates, he'd disappeared, too. The supply closet door was open. The classroom was empty, except a few stray yarn skeins scattered across the floor. They'd cleaned her out again.

wwww

Miriam paused at her classroom door. A right turn would lead to Mr. Kalt's office. To her left were the metal doors to the schoolyard. That morning, she'd heard Mr. Kalt bawling out a teacher who hadn't requested a substitute a week beforehand, as policy dictated. "Today of all days," he'd spat. Miriam didn't know what made today so special except for it being May Day, and as it happened, a day when she thought of her mother because of their shared May Day ritual. But Miriam had cunningly planned her party on top of the old memories. From now on, when this day arrived, as it would year after year with insulting regularity, Miriam would remember only the sweet smiling faces of her young charges circling the May Pole, the yarn twirling up in a parti-color cyclone. Then Miriam could live another year. Maybe, even, during the ceremony, the sky would open, or the ground, and she'd receive a sign of absolution from her mother. She'd even settle for Dad.

The children's disappearance reminded Miriam of a strange moment one morning when she was little. She'd awoken convinced that she had died during the night and was now a ghost, unable to be seen or heard ever again and forced to haunt the family's house while life continued around her. When the sensation struck, Miriam leaped out of bed and ran, yelling, "Mommy, mommy!" Miriam was a little disappointed when her mother said, "What is it, baby girl? I'm here." Even back then, she'd wanted to disappear.

The students had to be somewhere, though, not doomed to a strange netherworld of shoves and armpit farts just beyond her sight. More likely, they had succumbed to the lead that Miriam was now certain laced the drinking water and fouled the soil around Culvert, and she would stumble across them in a moaning blueberry-hued pile.

She veered left, toward the exterior doors. The loss of twenty-eight students would likely spur more yelling from Mr. Kalt, or worse. If she could just gather the students before anyone noticed their absence, everything would be fine. So long as the students kept mum. Maybe she could bribe them with something they liked. Glue sticks or a video of violent sports bloopers.

She pushed against the door, but the wind sealed it so firmly that Miriam had to lean against the crash bar with all her weight. She burst out into the air. Her skirt hugged her thighs. She squinted against the flying dust. The sky to the east looked clear, but behind her, a wall of dark clouds boiled. Great. Another storm.

The only place where students could hide on school grounds was behind the cottage where art classes were held. It was the site of the tetherball pole, or in a few short hours, the May Pole. Of course they'd gather there.

As Miriam rounded the side of the cottage, she spotted the students huddled together, the wind buffeting their light T-shirts. Such relief. But then she got angry. The students knew they weren't supposed to run away, yet they had, en masse. She couldn't even teach them how to play heads up seven up. And she got angrier when she considered that her first emotion had been fear of Mr. Kalt. The wrath of Kalt. Why should she have to worry about being disciplined when the students behaved with such gross impunity?

"What are you all doing out here?" Miriam shouted into the wind.

"Mr. Kalt told us to go stand by the May Pole," Cy said. A hooded sweatshirt dangled by its hood from the top of the pole, and several of the students were throwing the tetherball in an attempt to detach it. The rope kept altering the ball's trajectory, and none of the students were quite strong enough to heave the ball high enough.

"Don't lie to me," Miriam said. The students clustered around the pole. Miriam noticed that her yarn was spread across the ground behind them. She caught Jericho's eye. He stood with his hands behind his back like he'd been handcuffed. He smiled and ducked his head, as if to say, Welp, you got us.

"Let me try," Miriam said. The sweatshirt on top of the pole was Tuxton's. He wore it in all weather and liked to chew the cords on the hood, so they stiffened from his dried spit.

Tuxton stood apart from the group. "There's a tornado coming," he said. "I have to get inside."

He ran back toward the school while the other students laughed. "Duck and cover, Tuxton!" Jericho shouted after him.

"Were you torturing Tuxton?" Miriam asked.

The students blinked up at her with their red-rimmed eyelids, like bottom-dwelling fish dazzled by surface light. The wind shifted to a higher gear, from a bellow to a whine.

Miriam grasped the tetherball, took a few steps back, and shot it in a rainbow arc to the top of the pole. The hoodie floated to the ground. She was so pleased with her athleticism and tickled by her show of strength that it took a minute to notice Jericho had drawn a baseball bat from behind his back.

Just as Miriam opened her mouth to command him to give her the bat, to lay out clear boundaries as R and R recommended, Kimmy Schneider rammed Miriam from behind, knocking her onto the paved circle. Miriam's chin hit the asphalt first, her hands only partially breaking her fall. A veil of pain hazed between Miriam and the students, a swimmy space that dissolved into a miasma of nausea. The gray veil lifted as Miriam raised a palm to her chin and saw the red on her hand, felt the slick split flesh and the blob of fat and the hard edge of bone.

She started to cry. After all those days when she felt like weeping in front of her students but held firm. Her face was gone, her pretty young face, and her classroom management was shot. All she really wanted was her mother to gather her up and rock her and stroke her hair.

Miriam rose to her knees and tried to stand. The concrete stung the wounds on her palms.

Jericho brought the bat down on Miriam's back. She squealed and dropped again. She rolled so she could face him. His eyes, white blue and close-set, held no pity and no kindness.

"Please," Miriam said. She clasped a hand against the throb of her spine. The students gathered in a ring around her, their faces distorted. Miriam had never looked up at them before. Only down. Some students laughed, others shuffled their feet. Jericho smiled. The seconds dilated beyond all logic, with only the nearing storm to ground them in time—the moody clouds at the horizon, rolling in fast, the wind ratcheting up its pitch.

A thick band of lightning split the sky to the west and the students descended. Miriam screamed and flailed and rolled, dodging their size-two sneakers, their tight jabbing fists. She saw an opening in the melee. She rose to her knees and dove. She was nearly free when Cy yanked her down from behind, twisting her high heel like the horn of a bull. "Yeehaw!" he said.

There were simply too many students. She could have fended off two or maybe even five, if Kimmy weren't there, but Kimmy was there, and the students numbered twenty-eight. They closed in a circle around her, dancing like fairies, like furies. Miriam sat with the tetherball pole against her back for a little protection. The blood from her chin drenched the front of her blouse. Each breath hurt more than the last. Far away past the cottage, in the windows of the school building proper, Miriam swore she saw the curly white heads of her colleagues. When she looked again, they were gone.

"Remember how we played softball?" Miriam said, her voice high and wavering, her pathetic voice the therapist hated. "Wasn't that fun? Remember the multiplication tadpole? Don't you remember? We did so much art. I bought paint with my own money. You don't want to wreck May Day, do you?" Miriam asked. She spit a tooth into her palm and waved it above her head, as if that might change their minds.

Jericho pressed Miriam's back against the pole and several other students pulled her arms behind her. They wrapped her wrists tightly with the yarn. Miriam weighed the chances that her colleagues would save her. She struggled hard against her bonds. The yarn, which was extremely high quality, held firm.

But the students lost interest in her, as they had so many times before. Several got into a wrestling match, and another group played keep-away with a ball of sport weight merino. The largest batch of kids stared blankly toward the school, and behind it, the approaching storm.

The root of Miriam's tooth felt sharp in her hand. She wondered if she might use it to saw at the yarn that bound her wrists.

Too late. The students parted and Miriam tilted her head up to see a grownup approach. Her heart beat fast. It was none other than Mr. Kalt, who'd surely free her. They'd all rush into the school and wait out the storm and postpone May Day. Miriam herself would pack what remained of her possessions into the station wagon and hightail it back to her dead parents' house. Grief finds you, no matter where you hide. That was a lesson.

But something was wrong. Mr. Kalt spoke sternly, even a little unkindly—the voice he used as he handed down an out-of-school suspension: "We moved the party time up just a tick. Hope you don't mind." Mr. Kalt's mustache danced even more dramatically than usual, the ends actually peeling up from his face until finally, with a huff, he ripped it away entirely. Suddenly, her landlord Karl stood before her. Her landlord Karl in Mr. Kalt's suit with slicked-back hair and loafers shining.

"You knew all this time, didn't you?" Mr. Kalt said in Karl's voice, which must have been his real voice. "You had to have known. Just like you figured out the downside of our prime economic driver."

"Knew what?" Miriam asked.

"That we are one and the same! Mr. Kalt and Karl. Karl and Kalt, Kalt and Karl!"

"No," Miriam said. "I never did. Isn't that funny? I worked with you every day, and I couldn't see it. I was more interested in the pollution from the battery factory."

"Yes, that," Mr. Kalt said. He fingered the gluey pieces of his mustache in his palm.

"It's lead, isn't it? Tell me it's lead," Miriam said, trying to angle her head up so she could meet his eyes. "In the ground, the water, the air."

"Of course it's lead," Mr. Kalt snapped.

"You're sacrificing your children for money," Miriam said. "Then you don't even do anything interesting with the money. You buy big trucks, custom hunting stands."

"Abatement is pricey," Mr. Kalt said. "And you're sounding a mite judgmental. I'd suggest you review page 66 of the R and R handbook, little missy. The section on cultural differences."

"What parent would trade their child's IQ for a little money?" Miriam asked. "What adult?"

"You aren't a good teacher," Cy called from behind Mr. Kalt.

"You're developmentally delayed," Miriam said.

Mr. Kalt laughed hard. "Sometimes in an argument, both parties are right. Let that be a lesson to you, son.

"Miriam—Miss Green. We thought perhaps we might save a bit of money by trading out Mrs. Winkler for a cheaper model, maybe use that savings to hire a speech therapist for these kids who so badly need it, but then you had to go and fuck it up. Don't quote me on that, kids! That's adult talk."

"I thought you were my friend," Miriam said. She started crying again. The other teachers were filtering down to the tetherball pole. They led by the arms another woman with some sort of sack on her head.

"I heard what your little friend said about me on your voicemail," Mr. Kalt said. "Your 'perverted landlord.' Those words hurt."

"She said it, not me," Miriam said. It was the sort of excuse her students might use. Unconvincing. Miriam didn't have the wherewithal now to explain that, while she'd found Karl distinctly creepy, she had in fact grown to like Mr. Kalt. Miriam gasped. Her tooth, with which she had made some actual progress at cutting the yarn that bound her, skittered out of her grasp.

The other teachers reached the group. One of them carried the cardboard carton that held Miriam's family's ashes and the torn pages of the R and R handbook. A particularly brisk gust blew away a few pages. The woman with them had her hands bound behind her. Just like Miriam. The sack over the woman's head, Miriam could tell now, was Miriam's Rural and Rising tote.

Mrs. Sheldrake tugged the tote bag from the woman's head. It was Mrs. Winkler, whose bony body looked even frailer than when Miriam had seen her last. She had trouble standing against the buffeting wind.

"Should we go ahead, Mr. Kalt?" another teacher asked. "None of the community members are here yet."

"We'd planned something much grander," Mr. Kalt explained to Miriam and Mrs. Winkler. "We'd have filled the bleachers." He grasped the structure he'd built and wiggled it. A plank fell off. He kicked the loose board under the risers.

Mrs. Winkler stumbled down beside Miriam. They leaned against each other.

"My God, your face," Mrs. Winkler said.

"I'm sorry," Miriam said.

"Me, too," Mrs. Winkler said. "I thought the oils were helping. Soothing everyone down."

At Mr. Kalt's signal, the students each grabbed a hank of yarn, in every color of the rainbow. Mr. Kalt tied each strand near the top of the pole and set the students to work. They sang their May Day song and danced around the pole, just as Miriam had pictured, but she had trouble enjoying the performance because the yarn was tightening with each pass. Soon she couldn't get a full breath. The strands compressed her ribs.

"Are you okay?" she called to Mrs. Winkler. There was no response. When Miriam turned her head, just barely because the lashings held her neck, she saw Mrs. Winkler's head had sagged on her chest.

The students wrapped and wrapped the yarn around the May Pole they'd fashioned so cunningly using only their imaginations.

Cy paused to ask Mr. Kalt, "Can we put her in a barrel?"

Kalt replied, "Not just yet. The fire first, then we'll pack her up and tip her in the hog lagoon."

The sky had sickened to the green-yellow hue of twisters. The siren atop the school roared over the keen of the wind. The clouds streamed forward, punctured by dashes of lightning. Miriam tried to pick out shapes in the vaporous mass, to spot the beginnings of the end. A few feathery nubbins of fog plucked delicately down for mere seconds only to suck back into the main mass, which roiled purple-black. At last, the world hurts like I do, Miriam thought. A pathetic fallacy, her literary training reminded her. The clouds didn't care a whit for her sorrows.

"Hurry, hurry," urged Mr. Kalt. The teachers stuffed pages of *Teaching Is Learning* all around Miriam and Mrs. Winkler—under their knees, in their armpits.

"What should I do with these?" a teacher asked, holding up the three knotty pine boxes containing Miriam's family's ashes.

"Keep them with me," Miriam said.

The teacher shrugged and wedged them between Miriam's legs. Mr. Kalt struck a match. Jericho would get his wish. The May Pole would burn. Mr. Kalt stabbed the match around the crumpled paper and threw it right in the center of the pile. The wind thundered like a fully laden Mack truck. Everyone except Miriam and Mrs. Winkler clapped their hands over their ears.

"Look!" Mrs. Sheldrake said. Behind the school, a thin finger of cloud reached down toward the earth. Teachers and students all paused to gape as the finger grew into a thumb, then a whole arm.

Mr. Kalt grabbed a thick handful of matches, scraped the heads against the box, and threw the lit matches at Miriam. He turned tail and sprinted for the shelter of the school. He easily outpaced the teachers, who didn't pause a moment for Miriam's students, trailing at the back of the pack.

Most of the matches blew out, but a lit match ignited a wad of paper right at Miriam's armpit. A tickle turned to a prickle. The prickle turned to a sting. Wind fanned the flame. The axis mundi broke the back of the world. The May Pole at her spine formed a divining rod that would guide her to the bosoms of her dead beloveds. Miriam accepted the void's gifts. The tornado split in two. Each funnel widened, dancing with its twin. The turbid air bellowed and charged the women on the pole, a bee-stung bull unfathomably big and strong.

"Nothing's ever perfect. Have you noticed that?" Miriam asked Mrs. Winkler, who was beyond response. That had been one of her mother's sayings, infuriating for all its truth. Miriam never did tell her mother how much the saying annoyed her. It doesn't mean anything! Miriam would have liked to have shouted right in her dead mother's face. Of course nothing's perfect! Or maybe everything is! Have you ever thought of that? Miriam knew one thing: between the wind and the flame, there was nowhere for her to go but up.

Coda:
Waiting by
the Shore

THE CRUISE LINE HAD LOVED Elizabeth's ad agency's work on their European Adventure campaign so much that they'd offered her four days and three nights free. Elizabeth and the other three thousand passengers on the *Aria of the Tides* would disembark from Fort Lauderdale and cruise to Saint Kitts and Saint Lucia. She'd asked to go on the *Regal Adventuress*, the ship that steamed up the Rhine, but they'd balked because the river cruises cost much more.

A few weeks before Elizabeth left, Miriam's old neighbor Patty had called to see if Elizabeth wanted Miriam's ashes: "I've had her in my spice cabinet, but I thought it would be nicer if she went to a friend her own age." Her son, Clay, was headed to D.C. to intern with a congresswoman and could pass Elizabeth the box.

Elizabeth met Clay at a piano bar called Keyed Up in the middle of the afternoon. She picked the venue precisely because Chef Dave would have found it appalling—the candy-colored cocktails, the show tunes, the stained-glass lampshades above each high top. Based on Clay's name, Elizabeth had imagined a young Republican in a shiny-buttoned blazer, but Clay wore a striped Comme des Garçons T-shirt Elizabeth remembered coveting for herself during a monthlong tomboy phase when she'd chopped jeans into jorts and rode a longboard to a class called Moral Reasoning: If There Is No God, All Is Permitted.

Clay smiled apologetically, as if he didn't want to intrude on Elizabeth's sadness. The piano player, a very small old woman on a pedestal ringed by ferns, hammered out a baleful "Wichita Lineman."

"This one's an Arpeggio, and this is a Glissando," Elizabeth said, gesturing at a yellow and a blue cocktail sweating on the table. "You choose."

Clay pulled the blue liquid close. The piano transitioned to a bluesy "Somewhere Over the Rainbow." Clay and Elizabeth were the only customers. The bartender polished bottles with a white cloth. He sighed.

"We'll tip well," Elizabeth called. "So, Clay. You grew up with Miriam."

"I did," Clay said. "We lived next door. When we were little, we'd play school, and she was always the teacher. She'd mark right answers wrong on my quizzes to see if I was paying attention. Mostly she liked the red pen."

"That's funny," Elizabeth said. "That sounds like her." It didn't, though. The Miriam that Elizabeth had known would have let wrong answers slide.

"What was she like in high school?" Elizabeth asked.

"I don't like to think about high school," Clay said. "It wasn't a good time for me."

"You didn't get that shirt in Kansas," Elizabeth said.

"Actually, I did," Clay said. "It's a knockoff. It took two months to ship from China. The bottom seam is crooked, so I have to keep it tucked."

"Globalism," Elizabeth said.

"Right," Clay nodded. "Anyway, this is awkward." He held up a bulging canvas tote bag, singed black at the corners.

Elizabeth took the bag and peered inside. The bag smelled like a bonfire. She withdrew a pine box, too big to fit in her palm. The pianist hit the opening chords of "Goodbye Yellow Brick Road."

The box was heavy, but wood weighed a lot. "Do you really think Miriam's in here?" Elizabeth asked Clay.

"I've read that pets get all mixed up together when they're cremated. So you might get part of your pet back, and bits of everyone else's. I would assume more care gets taken with humans." Clay stirred his second cocktail, a B Sharp.

"Well, the corpses are larger, so they can't fit more than one in the oven, I'd assume," Elizabeth said.

"What are we talking about?" Clay asked.

"I don't know," Elizabeth said. "I really don't."

"I'm just the delivery boy," Clay said. He shifted his weight to the front of the barstool. One foot out the door.

"I'm sorry I got morbid. Patty said you lost your father recently," Elizabeth said.

Clay sank back on the stool. "Don't be sorry. It wasn't so much a loss as an unburdening. For my mom and me," Clay said. He circled his straw to get the last few drops of the B Sharp. "It's weird you spend so much time with a person, then when they're gone, you don't even miss them."

"How about another drink?" Elizabeth said. "They have a scorpion bowl, but they call it Boogie-Woogie."

"You be well, Elizabeth," Clay said. He slipped off the barstool.

"Wait," Elizabeth said. "What should I do with Miriam now? What do you think, I mean?"

"It doesn't matter," Clay said. "We got her out of Kansas."

"I'm going on a cruise. I'll take her," Elizabeth said.

The first lonesome strain of "Home on the Range" followed Clay out into the bright sunlight. He hadn't even remarked on how Elizabeth had requested all Kansas-themed songs for their meeting. She paid for their drinks (Clay hadn't offered) and tipped the piano player. She slung Miriam over her shoulder and headed to the old cemetery one last time.

Elizabeth had first found the cemetery close to her apartment shortly after Miriam had died, when she'd go on long walks in sunglasses that hid her red eyes. All thin crooked headstones from the 1800s and wrought iron gates and weird little death cottages—crypts, the groundskeeper had called them. Real estate was so expensive here they seemed like a waste. Kansas hadn't had crypts. She could live in a crypt. Happily!

Elizabeth liked to read all the gravestones. Sometimes she sent friends pictures of gravestones if she found their names on them, especially an unusual spelling. She'd comment, too, on the decedent's lifespan: "Just eight years old! You're already doing better than her." Or: "Eighty-one! Still a long way to go before you sleep." Her friends would text back "LOL" or "Oh, wow" or a surprised emoji or nothing at all.

Certain inscriptions filled her with something joy adjacent, especially the most self-pitying: "How many hopes lie buried here!" Her favorite—so fitting that she planned it for her own apex-top stone of Tropical Green granite—in Copperplate Gothic font: "She hath done what she could." Didn't we all.

Once, Elizabeth had darted down a strange path to avoid the groundskeeper. The light was different here, dappled by the leaves of the trees, and the stones were older and more ornate. Lots of double stones marked "Mother" and "Father," which reminded her of Miriam's dead parents, and right in the middle of the line, beside a couple discolored and badly weathered granite lambs, she spotted it: a plain gray stone, straight top, straight ends, no name, even. Just an inscription: Waiting by the Shore.

She'd tried to take a photo but her phone battery died. She never found that gravestone again. She circled the cemetery every day, searching. A few stones had tipped over, so she tried to pry them upright and got kicked out by the groundskeeper. "Have some respect," he'd told her as he pulled the wrought iron gate shut. "Stop being weird." But she wasn't being weird. Just sad. It wasn't weird to be sad.

Today Elizabeth wore a long dark flowing dress made of linen, which suited the scene. Lately her wardrobe had run to modern windswept-moor wear. She'd even prepared a line she never got to use, since no one but the groundskeeper paid attention to her mooning in the fake wreaths. Her line was, Don't mind me: I'm in deep mourning. She had a response ready, too, when the imaginary interlocutor suggested she hang out in a more cheerful place: It's not morbid if it makes me happy.

Elizabeth wound for hours through the gravel paths. At each fork she chose the less familiar route. Waiting by the Shore. Why couldn't she find it? Her buzz was wearing off and a headache blossomed behind her eyes. The light faded from yellow to green to purple. Her knees were aching. She decided to give up.

At the cemetery exit, the hoarse caws of crows stopped her. Five large birds perched in a maple tree with budding leaves. A few dived to the ground. Elizabeth wended toward the crows, where she found the Mother and Father stones, the lambs, and then, hidden by a shrub that had leafed out in the last month, her and Miriam's stone: Waiting by the Shore.

The crows clustered in front of the stone. The wind shifted and she smelled a whiff of ripe decay. She edged toward the stone to take a photo, and the crows flapped back to their tree, revealed what they'd surrounded, a dead cat with orange fur.

Elizabeth held her breath as she took the picture.

She ran from the cemetery, Miriam swinging hopefully and helpfully at her shoulder. Miriam's message was clear. She wanted to come on the cruise. Or Elizabeth would find her during the cruise. Maybe Miriam's message wasn't so easy to grasp.

Weeks later, on the cruise ship, Elizabeth lifted Miriam in her pine box to the railing. The wind whipped Elizabeth's hair into her mouth. "See?" she said. "The ocean. Water, water everywhere, and luckily, plenty to drink. Am I right?" Miriam loved when Elizabeth amended the classics. Elizabeth intended to make this trip all about what Miriam loved. Then, when the time seemed right, Elizabeth would dump Miriam overboard. Heave ho, old friend. To the briny depths with ye. Yo ho ho, and yes, certainly, a bottle of rum.

In Elizabeth's other hand she clasped a tall flamingo-pink cocktail with a crown of pineapple fanned over strawberry slices like a fancy hat. The crushed ice stung her palm. A loud foghorn blew, which made her laugh, because it sounded exactly like a cartoon ship's horn. Who knew that the sound, like a fart autotuned way down, existed in reality? There was so much Elizabeth had to learn.

Elizabeth moved from the railing to a deck chair. Behind her, drunk women in their forties and fifties danced the Electric Slide perilously close to the swimming pool. A conga line of gravestones: "They loved to dance!" A man with a belly domed like a turtle shell diligently worked his way through a plate laden with shrimp cocktails. "Always the life of the party." Children shrilled from the wave pool. "Lilies gathered too soon." Elizabeth had imagined that the whole trip might be a little quieter, a little more dignified.

She set Miriam on a side table next to her empty drink. "So Miriam," she said, "drinks now or drinks later? Both? I agree. Did you know that employees on these ships frequently work ten- or twelve-hour days for scant wages? I never would have gone if the trip wasn't paid for." A waiter removed her empty drink and tried to pick up Miriam as well, but Elizabeth stopped him. She held her hand on his a second too long as she took the box back. He had pretty eyes. "Easy on the ice this time, please," Elizabeth told him.

Elizabeth balanced Miriam on her shoulder like a parrot. "I have to tell you about Chef Dave, Miriam. He's the reason I only packed one-piece swimsuits. Well, that's not fair. He's the reason I'm still alive to select a suit at all. He found me mostly exsanguinated on his splendid cowhide rug and saved me by clasping a hand towel to my torso until the ambulance arrived. Then he never called again, which was fair. Anyway, I nearly sprung for a Missoni tankini, secondhand, but then I said, 'Elizabeth, will you really wear it when the scar heals, or will you go straight back to triangle-cut bikinis?' I think we both know the answer."

The waiter, who had pouty lips in addition to his nice eyes, said his name was Manny and he only worked eight hours per day. "They treat the Americans better," he told her. Elizabeth's hand brushed his as she received the second big pink drink. This one hit harder than the first. Manny was good as his word about going easy on the ice.

Elizabeth cradled Miriam in the nook of her elbow. Poor Miriam. Burned up in a freak apartment fire during a tornado in the heart of nowhere. She cried quietly for a few minutes and pushed her large black sunglasses hard against her nose so no one could see the wetness underneath, a sort of reverse snorkel. "I miss you, friend," she said.

The water in the distance flushed the color of a new bruise. Waves filed across the sea in the same appallingly long lines as the fields of wheat back in Kansas. Elizabeth's arms were very cold, despite the sun. She shrugged her silky caftan over her shoulders like a royal cape. The blankness of the ocean, its vast empty horizon, sickened her. Elizabeth had never seen much ocean. Neither had Miriam. Clay's words returned: We got her out of Kansas. Elizabeth could not in good conscience distribute Miriam here in the wide wet prairie. That much was clear.

Here's what she did instead:

- Throw a handful of Miriam in the air right as a low-flying jet buzzed close to Elizabeth and other onlookers.
- Spread Miriam all over the lettuce used to feed the iguanas during the iguana-feeding outing. The iguanas gobbled her right down.
- Lick some quarters, dip them in Miriam, and play the slots at the casino. She won fourteen dollars.
- Load her into the confetti cannons at the disco.

Manny had a soft face, a sweet face, which surely belied a truly ripped body. He carried himself with grace and confidence, like a dancer. And they did dance, at the disco with the light-up dance floor after he helped her pack Miriam in the confetti cannon. Here Elizabeth was, back on the prowl. Did the whole process seem a little repetitive, a bit rote? It did not. Elizabeth had located one really great guy. She could find others and not bleed on anything expensive this time.

Manny danced well, unselfconsciously feeling the music with his whole body.

"I'm thirsty," Elizabeth shouted in his ear. "Want to get a drink?"

They settled into a table far enough from the dance floor that they could hear each other.

"So where are you from?" Manny asked.

"D.C.," Elizabeth said. "Kansas originally."

Manny smacked the table as if displaying a winning poker hand. "Me too," he said. "I knew there was something familiar about you."

"She was from Kansas, too," Elizabeth said, gesturing toward the confetti cannon.

"That's wild," Manny said. "I left at seventeen. Never been back."

"I read this story once where this couple meet on the *Titanic*, and she knows the boat will sink and he doesn't," Elizabeth said.

"Does she tell him?" Manny asked.

"She still got on the boat. Why would she do that?" Elizabeth said.

"Ship," Manny said. "Big boats are ships. You should know that if you write about them. Maybe she wanted to die."

"Do you ever get tired of yourself? Like your own body and your own bullshit?" Elizabeth said. "I mean, look at me. I look stupid. I look like a blow-up doll. Not like a Macy's float. A sex doll." She jerked her hand to indicate, and a pain from the scar shot up her side.

"What was it you said she said?"

"What?"

"On the grave."

"Oh, Waiting by the Shore?"

"Have you thought that maybe that message was a metaphor? Like you're separated by an ocean now, but it's like the ocean between life and death, and when you die, you'll find her waiting?" Manny said. The lights from the dance floor pulsed blue on half his face.

"What if the message was a trick to lure me on this ship, which will sink?" Elizabeth said.

"That's an elaborate trick," Manny said, "and kind of mean. She was your friend?"

"I thought she'd actually be at some port waiting for me, waiting and waving. Isn't that stupid?" Elizabeth said.

Manny said something, but it was too quiet. The bass pumped like a heartbeat.

"What?" Elizabeth said. "What did you say?"

"It's nice, doing this for a person you loved and lost. Doing this even though you don't know what you're doing."

He lay his hand on hers. It felt warm, smooth, and strong. He said, "Let's dance."

When Elizabeth and Manny parted the next morning, he took a vial of Miriam, which he promised to sprinkle on dry land at each port. "Keep an eye out, too," Elizabeth said. "If you see someone who looks familiar but you aren't sure why, please say, 'Hello, Elizabeth loves you,' just in case." Elizabeth had done what she could.

On the last day of the cruise, on the beach at Fort Lauderdale, Elizabeth set the box with the last crumbs of Miriam in the sand. Perhaps a very large hermit crab might find the box and use it in lieu of a seashell. Miriam had always loved animals, and Elizabeth imagined sheltering a crustacean in her afterlife would please Miriam. The crab could claw its way inside and make itself at home.

ACKNOWLEDGMENTS

Thank you to the following publications in which versions of these short stories first appeared: "Prairie Vision" in the *Cincinnati Review*, "The Moat" in *Copper Nickel*, "The Tunnel" in *New Ohio Review*, "Elegy for Organ in Ten Parts" in *The Lifted Brow*, "A New Man" in the *Cimarron Review*, and "Various Shortcomings of Mine" in *Cutbank*.

My sincere thanks to Roxane Gay, series editor, for her selection of this manuscript and helpful edits. Thank you to the editors and staff at the University of Georgia Press for their kind support in shepherding *Mad Prairie* to publication. The Hambidge Center and the Sundress Academy for the Arts gave me space to finish this project.

Thank you to Alison Ruch, Christina Bolinger, Sara Pritchard, Nicole Shawan Junior, Amanda Gomez, and especially Robert Long Foreman and Wendy Oleson for their wise editorial advice about this book.

I am lucky to have had remarkable teachers at Harvard, Oregon State University (best MFA in the country), and the University of Missouri: Suzanne Berne, Patricia Powell, Marjorie Sandor, Keith Scribner, Tracy Daugherty, Marly Swick, Maureen Stanton, and Trudy Lewis.

Thank you to the *Missouri Review* crew for the support, wisdom, and fun: Kris Somerville, Speer Morgan, Marc McKee, Dedra Earl, and Evelyn Somers. The *Missouri Review* is a gem at the University of Missouri.

I have been uniquely blessed to work with creative and inspiring colleagues at Allegheny College and Worcester Polytechnic Institute, including Matthew Ferrence, Christopher Bakken, Kris Boudreau, Jim Cocola, Michelle Ephraim, Rebecca Moody, Mohammed El Hamzaoui, Lindsay Davis, Yunus Telliel, and Shana Lessing.

And thank you to my friends, near and far—I wish you all were near: Clarice Crawford, Stefanie Wortman, Meagan Ciesla, Joanna Luloff, Will Buck, Christina Ingoglia, Dave Nykodym, Takken Wish, Stephanie Wish, Gary Garrison, Mindy Burkhardt, Danny Miller, Shannon Calderone, Christine Yokoyama, Andrew Goulet, and the Powerful Island Team.

I am so grateful for the loving support of my family, Nancy and Ray Aguilar, Steve Aguilar, John McIntyre, and Pam McIntyre.

Most of all, thank you to Joe Aguilar, my collaborator in art and life. Every year I love you more. How is that possible?

The Flannery O'Connor Award
for Short Fiction

ANNIVERSARY ANTHOLOGIES

TENTH ANNIVERSARY

The Flannery O'Connor Award: Selected Stories, edited by Charles East

FIFTEENTH ANNIVERSARY

Listening to the Voices: Stories from the Flannery O'Connor Award, edited by Charles East

THIRTIETH ANNIVERSARY

Stories from the Flannery O'Connor Award: A 30th Anniversary Anthology: The Early Years, edited by Charles East

Stories from the Flannery O'Connor Award: A 30th Anniversary Anthology: The Recent Years, edited by Nancy Zafris

THEMATIC ANTHOLOGIES

Hold That Knowledge: Stories about Love from the Flannery O'Connor Award for Short Fiction, edited by Ethan Laughman

The Slow Release: Stories about Death from the Flannery O'Connor Award for Short Fiction, edited by Ethan Laughman

Spinning Away from the Center: Stories about Homesickness and Homecoming from the Flannery O'Connor Award for Short Fiction, edited by Ethan Laughman

Rituals to Observe: Stories about Holidays from the Flannery O'Connor Award for Short Fiction, edited by Ethan Laughman

Good and Balanced: Stories about Sports from the Flannery O'Connor Award for Short Fiction, edited by Ethan Laughman

Down on the Sidewalk: Stories about Children and Childhood from the Flannery O'Connor Award for Short Fiction, edited by Ethan Laughman

A Perfect Souvenir: Stories about Travel from the Flannery O'Connor Award for Short Fiction, edited by Ethan Laughman

A Day's Pay: Stories about Work from the Flannery O'Connor Award for Short Fiction, edited by Ethan Laughman

Growing Up: Stories about Adolescence from the Flannery O'Connor Award for Short Fiction, edited by Ethan Laughman

Changes: Stories about Transformation from the Flannery O'Connor Award for Short Fiction, edited by Ethan Laughman